"Jess," She Whispered.
"No . . ."

But his hands slid up to her shoulders, then to her back, pulling her toward him, removing those last inches of separation. Her bare thighs touched his, and fire licked through her nerve ends.

She knew, with a certainty that carried a special element of panic, that he was about to kiss her.

"No, Jess," she repeated, this time with more conviction. "This is total insanity. We only met a few hours ago."

He nodded. "Yes, I know. It happens that way sometimes, doesn't it? Chemistry or something between a man and a woman. I think I wanted to kiss you that first minute I saw you in the hotel lobby. You felt the same."

PATTI BECKMAN
has lived the exciting life of many of her heroines. She has been an actress, airplane pilot, author and bass player in her husband's jazz band. For this story she drew on first-hand knowledge of popular music and Nashville. She lives in Texas with her writer-musician husband and daughter.

Dear Reader:

Romance readers have been enthusiastic about Silhouette Special Editions for years. And that's not by accident: Special Editions were the first of their kind and continue to feature realistic stories with heightened romantic tension.

The longer stories, sophisticated style, greater sensual detail and variety that made Special Editions popular are the same elements that will make you want to read book after book.

We hope that you enjoy this Special Edition today, and will enjoy many more.

The Editors at Silhouette Books

PATTI BECKMAN
Nashville Blues

Silhouette Special Edition

Published by Silhouette Books New York

America's Publisher of Contemporary Romance

SILHOUETTE BOOKS

Copyright © 1985 by Patti Beckman
Cover artwork copyright © 1985 Franco Accornero

Distributed by Pocket Books

ISBN: 0-373-09001-3

First Silhouette Books printing January, 1985

10 9 8 7 6 5 4 3 2 1

Map by Ray Lundgren

SILHOUETTE, SILHOUETTE SPECIAL EDITION and
colophon are registered trademarks

America's Publisher of Contemporary Romance

Printed in the U.S.A.

BC91

Books by Patti Beckman

Silhouette Romance

Captive Heart #8
The Beachcomber #37
Louisiana Lady #54
Angry Lover #72
Love's Treacherous Journey #96
Spotlight to Fame #124
Daring Encounter #154
Mermaid's Touch #179
Forbidden Affair #227
Time for Us #273

Silhouette Special Edition

Bitter Victory #13
Tender Deception #61
Enchanted Surrender #85
Thunder at Dawn #109
Storm Over the Everglades #169
Nashville Blues #212

Nashville
Blues

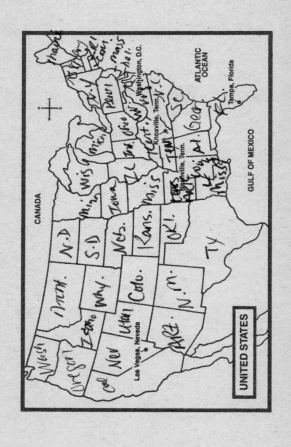

Chapter One

The Florida day was beautiful, a contrast to the emotional storm raging inside Andrea Castille. At the Tampa International Airport, she automatically made her way through the security check aisle, her mind elsewhere. The grating bleat of the loudspeakers calling her flight was a file against her strung-out nerves.

Sunlight, a glaring reflection from the silver body of the giant 747, momentarily blinded her, bringing her back to the reality of her surroundings. She drew a deep breath as if to brace herself.

Nothing of her inner turmoil showed as she climbed the stairs to the smiling hostess standing in the doorway of the plane. To the onlooker, she was as casually and naturally chic as the hostess herself. Above her comfortable midheel Capezios, her trim ankles and curving calves were attractive flashes as she stepped into the jetliner.

Inside, she drew a full share of male glances sparked with the hope that the black-eyed, raven-haired beauty might occupy the adjacent vacant seat.

It happened that she had a window seat, next to an elderly man who reminded her vaguely of her grandfather, Manola Castille.

The worry she had tried to suppress about her grandfather trickled back into her conscious mind as she sat down, placed her overnight case under her seat and laid the manila envelope of press information about Jess Clark on her lap.

Under normal circumstances, Manola Castille himself would be making this vitally important trip. But the pressures and worries of his failing business had sapped his strength, so Andrea was going in his place. The responsibility of this distasteful mission rested heavily on her slender shoulders.

Palms clammy, hands very steady, she buckled up. She felt the spaces of the cavern about her. She always had the flickering disbelief that such a massive structure of tons of gleaming metal could actually float on a tenuous ocean of thin, invisible air.

She drew a steadying breath, wishing the pilot would get on about his business. She'd be okay, once the blasted thing was off the ground and on its way.

Then came the surge of power, the pressure of the seat against her back. A few minutes later, Tampa was a toy city falling away in a spreading panorama of bays and inlets. Tropical green vegetation lay to the east beyond St. Petersburg with the sun-diamonded Gulf of Mexico stretching to the western horizon. When they touched ground again she would be in Nashville, Tennessee, country-western music capital of the world. That thought brought a fresh wave of resentment.

The cause of much of that anger was represented in the photographs and publicity releases contained in the thick manila envelope in her hands. She opened the clasp and slipped out an eight-by-ten glossy photograph of Jess Clark. She momentarily lost touch with her surroundings as those haunting, piercing eyes flashed out of the picture. They were the eyes of a man who had seen all sides of life from bitter, raw poverty to the adulation of the crowd. Gripped by that moody, powerful gaze, she felt strangely and uncomfortably disturbed. With an effort, she drew her eyes toward the other features, the rugged face of a man who had spent years outdoors at hard, back-breaking jobs that tested a man's strength and endurance. Those years had given him powerful shoulders and a deep chest. But the strong hands that had once known the handles of axes and grubbing hoes now caressed the strings of a guitar, wringing from the instrument the songs that were putting him at the top of all the country-western charts.

There was no question that Jess Clark was all man, radiating raw, macho sex appeal even in his photograph. With a flush, Andrea had to admit that a woman could be fatally attracted to a man like him. But then she remembered the other things she had heard about him and the anger returned. The stories said he had left a trail of broken hearts on his way to country-western stardom. Rumors had it that he had an overpowering male ego that fed on women who adored him. Whether all that was true or just tabloid gossip she had no way of knowing for certain, nor did she care. But she was sure of one thing—the Castille guitars that had been exquisitely, lovingly crafted by her family for generations were meant for the hands of a classical artist, not a corn-fed, backwoods musician like Jess Clark. The fact that the only hope for the survival of Castille guitars was in the hands of such a man galled her.

"That your boyfriend?" the elderly man beside her asked casually.

His voice startled Andrea out of her reverie. Momentarily disconcerted, she blurted, "Oh, good heavens, no! This is a picture of Jess Clark, the famous country-western singer."

"Oh, yes," said the old-timer, adjusting his glasses. "Guess I should have recognized him. I didn't mean to be nosy, miss. You were staring at the picture so hard, I couldn't help noticing. Do you know Jess Clark personally?"

"Not exactly. I have to see him on business."

"That so! Say, maybe you could get his autograph for my nineteen-year-old grandson. He's one of the boy's idols." The elderly man rubbed his hand over a thick head of silvery hair. "That's why I'm going to Nashville, to hear my grandson play his first professional engagement. He's got his heart set on becoming a big star someday like Jess Clark, there."

"Well, I hope he makes it," Andrea said.

"I do too. Don't mind telling you the whole family has lost a lot of sleep over that boy. My daughter, his mother, had big hopes for him making something worthwhile out of his life, becoming a doctor or lawyer or something. Never had anything in his head but music, though. Got into all kinds of trouble at school. Finally just dropped out. Packed up his guitar and took off on his motorcycle.

Next thing we heard he was in Nashville trying to make it big like thousands of other kids who go there every year. Most of them leave disillusioned after a year or so. But maybe my grandson will be one of the lucky ones. He's got a lot of talent, I'll say that, and he's determined.''

"I guess that's what it takes," Andrea said. Was that what had gotten Jess Clark to the top? Unswerving determination? Fate? Luck? In the publicity releases, she read he had been the son of a coal miner who'd died when Jess was a boy. There had been years of a bitter fight for survival, working at odd jobs during the day, riding the rails, sleeping in culverts, playing in obscure little honky-tonks on weekends for a few dollars while dodging flying beer bottles during chair-smashing free-for-alls. Why had he made it while so many others failed? Did he have that extra measure of talent? She wasn't one to judge. She knew nothing about country-western music. She came from a world that was totally foreign to that of Jess Clark's. Her musical tastes had been nurtured on the symphonies of Beethoven, the rhapsodies of Schumann, the artistry of Segovia.

The Castille family name reached far back to the ancient aristocracy of Spain. Royal blood flowed in Andrea's veins.

For the remainder of the trip, she tried to put aside thoughts of Jess Clark. For a while she dozed. Suddenly she was awakened by her garrulous seat partner. "Well," he said, "ready for the roller coaster? We're about to land. And to think some dang fools enjoy this kind of thing!" He took a deep breath and obeyed the lighted sign to buckle his seat belt.

Andrea smiled at the elderly man and followed suit. She

looked out the window at the city below. Her first impression of Nashville was of a Lilliputian city caught in the snakelike bends of the Cumberland River with the green-and-brown checkerboard of the undulating mid-Tennessee landscape sweeping to far horizons. Her mind was caught up with the thought of the elderly man's grandson and the old man's obvious pride. Nashville was one of the world's glamour cities, but Andrea couldn't wait to get the endorsement contract signed and then book the earliest flight back to familiar faces and surroundings.

When the plane had landed and Andrea had gathered up her belongings, her seat companion courteously motioned her ahead. Impulsively she touched his hand. "Good luck to you and your grandson."

He smiled, nodded and they were separated by a stream of people.

Inside the terminal building she stopped short, hearing her grandfather's name on the speaker system. Andrea picked her way through the hurrying swarm to the information desk. A tall, dark-haired woman smiled at her.

"The announcement for Mr. Castille," Andrea said. "I'm his proxy, here in his place."

"Well, in that case the gentleman over there is waiting for him . . . for you." The clerk pointed through a break in the crowd at a huge man standing several feet away.

She was supposed to have been met at the airport by Jess Clark, but this man was definitely not Jess. He looked like a heavyweight wrestler. He was florid and totally bald. Puffing on a stubby cigar, he stood placidly lazy, but his clothing was a busy riot—barefoot sandals, orange slacks and a Hawaiian shirt worn with the tail hanging out and stretching across his ample girth.

It's no more than I should have expected, she thought sourly. Jess Clark had not proved the most reliable of contacts thus far. She guessed she was lucky he had remembered to send someone to meet her at all.

"Excuse me." Andrea cleared her throat. "Were you having Mr. Castille paged?"

He took the cigar from his thick-lipped mouth. "Sure was." His prominent brown eyes glanced up and down her slender frame, an automatic male response. His appreciation was frank but inoffensive. He gave her a big friendly smile. "You're certainly not a mister."

Andrea's first reaction to him melted into something resembling affability. He reminded her of a large, affectionate dog. She returned his smile. "Mr. Castille was unable to make the trip. I'm his granddaughter, and I'm here to represent Castille Guitars. My name is Andrea Castille."

He offered a big, warm mitt for a handshake. "It's a pure pleasure to meet you. My handle is Sloan. My friends call me Peewee. I'm keyboard in the Jess Clark collection of misfits, outcasts and renegades."

Andrea tried to suppress a chuckle. A man his size named Peewee? She couldn't imagine that man-mountain mass and those frankfurter fingers at an organ or piano. But then walking along the street, famed violinist Isaac Stern didn't look all that much like a violin virtuoso either.

"Jess sends his apologies for being too busy to welcome you in person."

She wanted to say it was no more than she had expected, but she didn't want to seem rude. "It's all right, Mr. Sloan," she replied.

"Peewee," he amended. "That mister stuff makes me uncomfortable."

Andrea smiled. "Peewee it is."

He dropped his stubby cigar in a sand-filled receptacle. "Would you like a drink or something?"

"Thanks, but I think I'd like to get to the hotel. I have to make a call to Tampa."

"Sure thing. We'll fetch your luggage and be on our way."

Minutes later she was sitting beside him in his somewhat startling car, a gleaming conservative black Lincoln with a pair of spreading longhorns ornamenting the front of the hood and an interior of wild zebra stripes. He slid the car from a ramp into the rush of citybound traffic with the deftness of one of those rare, perfectly coordinated big men. Despite his lazy air, his movements were as graceful as a dancer's.

"Where you registered?" Peewee asked.

"The Hyatt Regency."

"Very nice." Peewee nodded. "And right downtown, convenient to everything while you're with us. You've come to a one-of-a-kind city."

Peewee slowed and veered the big car onto a ramp. They were soon crawling along in the congestion of an old city street, past weathered gingerbread houses where a room-to-let sign occasionally showed. Nothing of the music city glamour was visible here. The scene outside the air-conditioned Lincoln's window might have been plucked from any of a half dozen old southern cities,

Charleston or Savannah, Augusta or Mobile. Or maybe not.

Maybe this was a street of the hopefuls that only looked like old decayed streets in other cities. Maybe it was a street of fantasies, dreams of fame and fortune, like those of the grandson of the man on the plane. Such kids could afford only a dreary room on such a street, the youngsters from a farm in Arkansas, a grubby village in Appalachia, a street in Richmond or Houston.

"Do you get a lot of young kids hoping to make it big coming to Nashville?"

"By the truckloads," Peewee said. "They arrive in rattling pickups, wheezing vans, on snarling motorcycles. A lot of them hitchhike. And all of them wear the same uniform—patched and faded jeans, shapeless T-shirts, long hair, eyeshades. Those poor little suckers arrive with guitars on their backs, belongings in duffel bags stuffed in the boot of a dented VW or tossed in the back of a battered heap. They look at the street without really seeing it because they don't want to. Loretta Lynn, Johnny Cash, Jess Clark, Dolly Parton . . . these are the truth of Nashville to the youth tired of greasing cars in Pensacola or the girl sick of slinging hash in Tulsa. They think they won't have to pound the pavement long looking for their dream come true before they hit it big. Somebody has told them they ought to be on the Grand Ole Opry. They can't see nothin' but a sky full of stars even if it's raining cats and rusty nails. Travel the path, make the rounds, budget the money so they can hit a lot of joints in one night and sit in on one of the jam sessions, where somebody who counts might hear them."

"And if nobody does?"

The large slope of his shoulders shrugged, rippling the wildly hued Hawaiian shirt. "Hang tough," he said, as if it had never occurred to him not to.

"What about the ones who aren't all that tough?"

"Guess they hock the guitar or sell the jalopy for the price of a bus ticket and never quite figure out why it didn't turn out for them like it did for Buddy or Hank senior and junior or Tammy."

"But then there are the handful who make it?" Andrea asked.

"Yep," Peewee responded. "And that's why they keep chasing that rainbow. Who knows which new kid in town is tomorrow's Skeeter Davis?"

This was all foreign to Andrea. "But you're one who made it, Peewee." It was as much a question as a statement.

"Sure enough. I'm playing with Jess Clark. You can't get much bigger than that. 'Course there was about seven years of playing for pass-the-hat and four-hundred-mile jumps between one-nighters for gas money to the next. Might have been seven more, if Jess Clark hadn't happened into Bodeen's one night and heard me play."

Andrea glimpsed the towering monolith ahead and guessed it was the Hyatt Regency. "Sounds as if that was your lucky night, Peewee."

He nodded thoughtfully. "Turned out to be that way. Luckiest night of my life. But that night when it happened was lucky for Jess, him getting a meal and a beer to wash it down. He opened that beat-up guitar case and took out that precious baby—it was an old secondhand instrument —and he says, 'What key do you play "Closer Walk" in?' And I says, 'Any key you want, buddy, they're all on the keyboard.' And he says, 'All right, we'll do our number in E flat.' "

Peewee was slowly edging the car toward the curb, in no hurry to end his story.

"So we did the number in E flat," he said, "and usually you can't hear yourself play in the beery clamor at Bodeen's joint. But when Jess started telling them the truth, that old firetrap got real quiet. And something happened that night between the guitar and the piano and that voice and the people. When Jess had sung the last note, finishing with the major seventh sound like he does sometimes, you could hear sink water dripping behind the bar. An old coot with tears running down his cheeks comes over and sticks a ten-dollar bill behind the E string on Jess's guitar. I says, 'You always sing that good?' And Jess says, 'I was a little thin on the high notes because of a condition of the stomach.' You see, he hadn't eaten since the night before. So the first thing he does is lay away three of Bodeen's hamburgers, two of which might have killed him on the spot. He said it was the most gosh-awful food he'd ever eaten, but it sure did push out a few uncomfortable wrinkles."

Peewee broke off as if suddenly self-conscious. Laughter wrinkles formed at the corners of his big, friendly eyes. "Now wasn't that some heck of a welcome to Nashville?"

Andrea was silent for a moment, at a loss for words, strangely moved by the story. Then she managed a light tone. "I guess I'll remember not to eat any hamburgers at Bodeen's!"

"Oh, the food's better now since Bodeen's wife took over the place. She's one of them goes in for crafts and such as a hobby. She made a big stained-glass sign for behind the bar that says, 'Jess Clark Sang Here.'"

He brought the car to a stop at last. A smartly uniformed doorman was already on hand to assist Andrea in alighting.

In parting, Peewee said, "I'll get hold of Jess and let him know he missed a fine treatment for the eyes at the airport."

Andrea's cheeks colored as she smiled. The Lincoln pulled away from the curb and Andrea's bags were whisked inside. The spacious lobby overwhelmed her. The ceiling seemed to rise to the very sky. The atrium garden was a fantasy in green. There were people and movement, but they didn't seem to disturb the sense of soothing quiet pervading the elegant surroundings.

The clerk made her feel as if the hotel had been waiting for nothing more or less than her arrival. She asked for the key and a few minutes later was tipping the boy who ushered her into a twentieth-floor room and checked the air conditioning, drapery pulls and ice water carafe. Her luggage, including a leather case containing a finely crafted Castille guitar, was carried in moments later.

The room was everything a visitor could ask for, plushly appointed and furnished to provide every creature comfort. The thick carpet felt soft beneath her feet as she kicked off her shoes and padded toward the bathroom. She stopped to check out the miles-long view from her window, looking toward and beyond the Grecian elegance of the state capital building. The Nashville music scene with its many spin-off attractions lured tourists and visitors in swarming thousands.

She turned from the window wanting the hours to pass quickly and hurry her through the task that had brought her here. She tried to imagine a correlation of Jess Clark's background and her own, some small point that would break the ice for discussion. It wouldn't work. Their worlds were a universe apart. Only the matter of Castille guitars was a link between them.

She had an aristocratic background that had begun in Spain centuries before she was born. Her great-grandparents had emigrated from Spain, bringing with them the fine tradition of guitar making that had made her family the toast of Spanish musical circles in the old country. She had felt pride from earliest childhood in her roots. She'd known nothing of the kind of circumstances that had shaped Jess Clark.

Born to a coal miner father who had died young and an ignorant slip of a malnourished gal-young'un, as his press releases called her, Jess grew up in a slab shack on a barren West Virginia mountainside. He'd gone down into the darkness and dangers of a coal mine at an age when youths of Andrea's circle were sharpening up their tennis and zipping around town in their MGs. One glorious Christmas an uncle, who sold odds and ends out of a wheezing pickup truck at the local flea markets, gave young Jess a battered secondhand guitar. The repercussions, Andrea reflected, were eventually to echo across the nation.

When her grandfather had opened negotiations with Jess Clark, his had been a remote name to her. Popular with the country-western crowd, he was far removed from her musical tastes. In ensuing days, as stories, articles, PR material and research notes cluttered her desk, she came to know more about him than some of the boys she'd grown up with. But the essence of the man remained a mystery.

She couldn't, for example, experience one of those weekends in the poverty-stricken region when men came from the bowels of the earth to rediscover the sunshine until the following Monday morning, as Jess had done.

The Castilles had been guitar makers for centuries, their fine instruments the choice of the best classical guitarists. After the family emigrated to the United States, they carried on their tradition of building quality guitars.

The offices and factory of Castille Guitars occupied an old loft building in Ybor City, a bit of old-world Spain adjacent to early downtown in Tampa, Florida. It was here that Manola Castille, Andrea's grandfather, had poured more than forty years of loving care into the manufacture of his beautiful instruments.

Since she was a child, the factory had been a second home to Andrea. She loved the homey atmosphere and the subdued sounds of old-world craft. The factory sprawled beyond the office corridor. There were the long tables and overhead trolleys, the permeating smell of glue and fresh wood sandings, the array of guitars in every stage of completion. Finally, when they were complete and tested, always under Manola's critical eye, the instruments were boxed and loaded on the freight elevator in the far rear for warehousing at street level and shipping from a loading dock on the busy street behind the building.

The factory gave Andrea a timeless sense of steady but unhurried activity aimed always at quality in production. Most of the denim-aproned craftsmen were older men, a few with bushy iron-gray mustaches who made Andrea think of benign uncles who contemplatively smoked curved Wellington pipes.

They were busy at a multitude of tasks, cutting fine spruce, rosewood, mahogany, teak. Bending, shaping, gluing, clamping. Polishing mother-of-pearl inserts between frets. Mounting turning pegs lathed from Manola's own alloy in a design that could keep a Castille in tune indefinitely.

Always, her grandfather hovered over the operation. Since childhood she had affectionately called him by the Spanish name for grandfather—*abuelo*. With his shock of hair and fierce handlebar mustache snow white against his mahogany complexion, he was somehow much more Abuelo than Grandfather. He was indelibly engraved in her memories of the place: Abuelo picking up a thin sheet of planed spruce and showing her how to read the grain; Abuelo with a droplet of lacquer between thumb and forefinger, demonstrating to her the old-master way of checking viscosity by seeing how many thousandths of an inch the liquid would stretch; Abuelo's marvelous hands, long, tapered fingers darting like serpent tongues, testing a new guitar with full-string flamenco fire or incredibly counterpointed passages from a composer like Ravel.

That had been Andrea's life, her background, her culture. Now the security and way of life she had known was threatened.

God love him, Abuelo was something of a stranger in today's economic environment. It was a ball game he had never quite learned to play. He was a man from an era of ledgers and spindle files, of infinite care in craftsmanship and inventory and cost control by piecemeal counting. He had little affinity for computerized complexities, mass assembly and cheap, synthetic materials. He scorned the shiny shoddiness of many guitar brands flooding the market from overseas and from American manufacturers who farmed out to low-wage labor and merely stenciled their names on the end products.

But it took more than old-world craftsmanship to keep abreast of today's market. The Castille company had been losing money for several years, steadily eroding Manola Castille's resources, both financial and physical. Andrea's grandfather had become baffled, depressed.

Raymond Ayers, the bright young manager Manola had taken into the company, got the idea of capturing a new market through the award-winning country singer, Jess Clark. He had to explain to Manola who Jess Clark was. "His appearance can fill the Superdome," Raymond argued. "His endorsement, his name, will sell guitars. Castille guitars! Jess Clark is a classicist in his genre, no less an artist in his field than Montoya or Liona Boyd. He would never lend his name to a shoddy product. We'll leave the discount store trade to others. If Jess Clark picks up a Castille guitar every time he performs and if he agrees to let us use his name in our promotions, we'll have every country singer in the nation buying our instruments."

There had begun a tedious dickering with Jess Clark's business manager. Yes, the Clark organization was interested. Trying to pin him down to a written agreement was another matter. The Nashville balladeer had shown no desire to expedite the matter or even, at times, to cooperate. Manola had raged and stewed. Maybe the ex-hillbilly's life was now that of a busy, sought-after star. But the linking of a name, even the name Jess Clark, to the fine old name of Castille Guitars wasn't exactly an invitation to a backwater corn-husking, Abuelo had fumed.

Clark had subjected them to one irritating delay after another. Finally, there appeared to be a general agreement on the terms. Manola Castille was to meet Clark in Nashville with the papers. That was another blow to the old man's dignity. He would have swallowed his pride and made the trip, but his doctor warned that the strain might be too much for his tired old heart. Raymond Ayers could have gone, but Jess Clark stubbornly refused to deal with anyone but a member of the Castille family. That left Andrea to carry the all-important papers to Nashville. With her parents dead, Manola Castille was her only family. For the old grandfather's sake, she had agreed to take on the disagreeable task.

Andrea knew if the company failed, it would be the death of her beloved Abuelo Castille. She knew that somehow she must deal with this man, Jess Clark. The prospect of meeting him face-to-face was strangely unsettling and disturbing.

The soft ring of the phone interrupted her thoughts.

"Hello," she said.

"Miss Castille," came a rich baritone voice. "This is Jess Clark."

She felt a strange shock. Until now Jess Clark had been a name, a legend. This was the real voice, the real person. She found herself momentarily speechless.

He continued, "Peewee Sloan briefed me on your arrival. Sorry it was less than red carpet. I'm down in the lobby. If you can come down, I'll apologize in person."

Andrea was surprised by the civilized quality of his

speech. She'd expected him to sound like a hillbilly. At last she found her voice. "That's not necessary," she said with stiff politeness.

"I know it's short notice, but we usually have to move that way in these parts. So if you can come down now, I'll show you some of the sites while we talk business."

I'm not here as a tourist, she thought. But she said, "That would be nice. Thank you. I'll be right down."

She hung the phone in the cradle. There now. Her intentionally businesslike tone was the note on which she intended to conduct this deal. Efficiently, quickly. Get his signature and return to Tampa where she belonged. But she felt much less composed than her cool voice implied. Her emotions were scattering in all directions. What was wrong with her? Surely she couldn't be getting stage fright at the prospect of meeting a famous country-western star! The very thought made her cheeks burn. No, it was something else. The memory of those piercing eyes that had stared out of his photograph flashed across her mind. It was the prospect of coming face-to-face with the living version that had unnerved her.

In the lobby it took only seconds to spot Jess Clark. He was signing autographs for a collection of giggling young girls dressed in tight blue jeans and loose western shirts. They must have followed him in off the street.

She approached him and stood on the edge of the tight knot of excited teenagers, waiting for him to finish. He flashed a young fan a broad grin and asked her name. Andrea realized he had spoken with a soft western drawl. *The fraud!* Andrea thought. *He puts on a country accent in person the way he does a cowboy hat. Just part of the image!*

His large hands swiftly scrawled on a sheet of paper the girl had handed him. He looked very much the country-western superstar in his shimmering cowboy shirt with dazzling gold fringe, hip-hugging jeans and expensive western boots. A rebellious lock of hair tumbled onto his forehead. His gaze turned in Andrea's direction.

Seeing him in real life brought a greater impact than she had bargained for. His face was too boldly hewn for the classically handsome mold. It made her think of a sculpture from which the traces of chisel and maul hadn't been entirely polished. The chin was blunt and square beneath a mouth almost generous in its width and fullness of lips. The cheeks were tanned, lean planes drawn downward from the convex curve of the stubborn cheekbones. Nose thin and straight. Dark-brown hair coarse and thick, neatly styled at earlobe length. The forehead was high, slightly creased with lines.

But those eyes! Yes, it was the eyes that stunned and weakened her. Dark, dark brown like the shadowy depths of a wild forest. And more. Things she had never seen in a man's eyes before; only eyes that had seen a glimpse of hell could have that haunted darkness. Only the compensating vision of a poet touched a soft light to the shadows.

The power of his gaze was almost overwhelming. Never in her life had she encountered such an electrifying personality. Now she could understand how he could bring an audience weeping and applauding to its feet.

"Miss Castille," he said, reaching out to grip her hand. The touch sent a vibrating current through every nerve of her body.

Chapter Two

$\mathcal{J}$ess Clark tried not to be too obvious in his survey of the young woman whose hand he had captured. But her beauty dazzled him. Against her mane of luxurious black hair, her skin was a creamy porcelain. Her enormous eyes matched the midnight depths of her hair. Her skillfully applied makeup was no more than a subtle emphasis of classic beauty, giving clean lines to winged brows, a hint of violet to eyelids and drama to long lashes. Her nose and cheekbones had a patrician elegance; lips were as inviting as lush fruit, throat long and slender. Her shoulders were squared, her breasts proud and straining against the stylish garments that caressed exquisite curves.

In a word, she was breathtaking.

The slightly haughty lift of her chin and the self-assured glint in her eyes reminded him that here was a woman of aristocratic breeding. He remembered with an inward smile Peewee's summation when he'd described the young woman he had picked up at the airport. "The dame's got class, Jess."

Yes, she definitely had class. He was not accustomed to dealing with this kind of woman. She could make a man downright unsure of what to say first.

Andrea thought his grip was politely gentle, but she could feel the pent-up, tensile power of his hand. It was like touching a switch and then realizing suddenly that it was a leash. The person who flipped the switch could release a blinding power.

Coolly, she slipped her hand free. Her mind fashioned the determined reminder that she wasn't interested in any of Jess Clark's switches. Obviously, there were plenty of women who were. She had just witnessed a demonstration of gushing, adoring female fans who had surrounded him.

But she was not about to join that parade. She was a businesswoman here with heavy responsibilities. He meant but one thing to her: a signature on the contracts of endorsement for Castille Guitars.

"Yes, I'm Andrea Castille," she responded to his greeting, angry at the involuntary thickness of her voice. "And you are Mr. Jess Clark."

"Guilty. Did you have a nice flight?"

"Very nice," she murmured, aware that this polite exchange was a kind of verbal fencing as they both tested the water to see how to proceed.

Her businesslike mien projected a coolness she didn't entirely feel. She couldn't ward off that intangible, indefinable effect of just being in his presence. In spite of all the things about him that made her resentful, she couldn't escape the raw, primitive truth that the man did have *it*—a kind of aura that imparted his maleness; his sexuality, like a subtle musk, emanated from him.

There was a lengthy moment of strained silence as they ran out of social clichés.

Then, with a lopsided grin, he asked, "Are you always so standoffish?"

"What do you mean?" she asked with a frown.

"No offense intended, Miss Castille." His grin widened. "But you're not very friendly."

"Well, I'm not here on a social visit. I'm here on business."

The corner of his mouth quirked and a sardonic expression was accentuated by a lifted eyebrow. Probably a lifelong reflex when something struck him as slightly amusing, she thought. Was he laughing at her?

She felt the flush of warm blood rising to her cheeks. Was he aware of the impelling effect the first moment of his presence had on her? Perhaps he took it for granted that any woman privileged with the touch of the great Jess Clark should react the same way, with a lurch of the heart, a breath pulsing in the throat.

What arrogance! First she had pegged him as a fraud. Perhaps arrogance was simply part and parcel of being a fraud.

Well, whatever he had seen, or thought he had seen, in her face and eyes, he could just stuff it in his guitar and twang it! Let his arrogance see what it would. She was here to do business, period.

He tried a new tack. "Would you like some refreshment after your trip?"

She dared look him full in the face once again. This

time she had the reassuring knowledge that her eyes were cool, detached. But inwardly she was still furious with herself, unable to shake the memory of the high-voltage electricity she had felt when he'd shaken her hand.

She weighed his invitation. She could hardly turn it down without appearing downright rude. It was, she thought with an inward sigh of resignation, part of doing business. Getting on a more relaxed, friendly ground with him might facilitate the matter she was here for. If she just wouldn't feel so self-conscious with him!

"Yes," she consented. "A drink would be nice while we discuss the contracts I brought along."

"What's the point in rushing things?" he asked with a smile.

"I would hardly call it rushing," she said coolly. "There was really no reason this appointment couldn't have been set weeks ago."

"And for the delay, I apologize, Miss Castille."

She shot him a surprised look.

"I really do," he said, smiling disarmingly.

His tone sounded sincere. He went on, "My business manager reads off the priorities. Unfortunately he rates other things more pressing at various moments."

"Such as?"

He moved those strapping shoulders in a slight shrug. "All the stuff that goes with the business I'm in. Haggling over a recording contract. Revising a schedule to include another one-nighter on a tour to the tune of several thousand dollars."

She could understand those things. Grudgingly, she had to admit that with his income, the stipend he was going to receive for endorsing Castille guitars was hardly going to put him in a higher tax bracket. She was on the point of relenting. Her full, lovely lips were about to form the words, "Your apology is accepted, Mr. Clark."

But then he rekindled her defenses by adding, "However, if I had been aware of the Castille delegate coming to see us, I would have personally overridden my business manager and given this appointment top priority!"

With a shock, she was again aware of that unnerving smokiness in his eyes. He was standing there as if the people in the awe-inspiring lobby didn't exist. There was no atrium garden, no cascading waterfall, no light coming down through a distant skylight set against the sky. There was only one focal point in the entire universe—Andrea Castille.

A little shred of fright touched her. To be looked at like that by a man could make any woman weak-kneed. Furiously, she marshaled her scattered thoughts. She was tired from the accumulated tension of the past days, the uncertainties, the worry over her grandfather's business. Her defenses were down. Under normal circumstances she wouldn't feel like a quarry at bay before those hypnotic eyes, she assured herself.

For a second she had been taken in by the sincere ring of his apology. But his added statement with its flirtatious implication had put him right back in character. He'd apologized for the wrong reason. Come to think of it, he'd apologized to himself for not making the appointment sooner now that he realized the sex of the Castille delegate.

What a colossal ego! And what else went with arrogance? He was what she'd expected from the very first, a man who had known humility in his impoverished boyhood, had had it crammed down his throat and then had turned it around and made up for it when the heady wine of success lifted him to the lofty heights of a celebrity. That was only human nature. Didn't they turn out the same way too frequently, the ragged boys or girls who achieved fame and fortune? Takes a lot of character to remember your beginnings and retain humility. Perhaps she shouldn't condemn him too harshly.

So that's the way I'm going to think of you, Andrea thought. Social forces had made him what he was. His arrogance was understandable, even warranting a note of pity.

She realized he was making a suggestion about the drink he had offered. "Right here in the hotel, we have three choices: the revolving lounge and restaurant, the window box cocktail lounge or a sidewalk cafe called The Troubador."

Andrea quickly assessed the choices. Already dizzy, she didn't want to be with him in a revolving lounge with its long, sweeping views of Nashville, his fiefdom, his domain. And the cocktail lounge sounded a bit too intimate.

"A breath of fresh air would be welcome," she said decisively.

He touched her elbow and despite the small warning of a tingle of pleasure she didn't shrug away. He had already accused her of being standoffish. She'd made her point, no need to overdo it.

Anyway, his touch was polite, a simple overtone of a quaint and old-fashioned courtesy. Something left over from that anachronism, the southern gentleman? She thought the arrogant fraud would probably stand up to give a seat to a little old lady on a city bus. Not that he'd use a bus. He moved about the Nashville streets, she was sure, in his choice of a Mercedes town car, plush station wagon or imported European sports car.

Seated facing each other in the lazy warmth of the Nashville day, he looked at Andrea questioningly while a pert waitress hovered nearby.

Andrea said, "A chilled white wine would do fine."

He nodded and glanced up at the waitress. "A bottle of—"

Andrea interrupted. "A small glass is all I want."

Again that infuriating quirk of the broad, firm masculine mouth dominated his expression; he looked like a cat toying with a mouse. What perverse turn of thought brought the flickering image of that mouth, lips parted, coming down on hers?

Disconcerted, she jerked her gaze from his lips and made a point of looking with mild interest at the passing scene, the unhurried flow of traffic, the movement of pedestrians at an intersection, the gawkers who pointed, whispered and stared at the great Jess Clark.

Predictably, a couple of girls had ventured closer on the sidewalk, covertly nudging one another and giggling.

Was there no escaping the aura of the first stupid, irrational, unexplainable moment when she'd gazed at him face-on in the publicity photographs?

Her stiffened shoulders relaxed slightly as the two girls moved on, continuing to slip backward glances. At least, Andrea thought with relief, they hadn't come to the table to fawn for autographs and look at her—if they bothered to see her at all—with murderous envy.

She heard him telling the waitress, "Two glasses of a white Bordeaux, Mouton-Cadet, 1980."

The waitress nodded approval of the vintage as she jotted down the order.

"Well, now." He quietly folded his large, blunt-fingered hands on the tablecloth before him as the waitress went for the drinks. "What would you like to see first in Nashville? You could spend months in this city and still not see everything. Perhaps I could give you a rundown of the places we might—"

"Your office, Mr. Clark, is the first place I should like to see. Your business manager and someone to notarize the endorsement contracts should be present. After that I'm afraid I must return immediately to Tampa."

"Tampa," he murmured, pointedly ignoring her stubborn adherence to the business at hand. "I was there once during the annual week-long Gasparilla festival when businessmen dress up as pirates and sail up the river to hoist the Jolly Roger over the City Hall. But all I saw of it was from an auditorium stage and the windows of the bus."

"Bus?"

"The big, customized job that gets me and my entourage from one concert to another. You just get passing glimpses when your schedule has you jumping from one stage to the next for, perhaps, a state fair appearance."

His voice trailed off. He realized this aristocratic young woman had no way of relating to the kind of life he was describing. She didn't know what he was talking about. She had never experienced the intoxicating thrill of standing before a stomping, whistling, crowd; the throat-tearing emotion of a song wrenched from the heart; the depression of pushing on even when you're half-dead with fatigue or aching with the flu or raw from a miserable cold in the vocal cords. Her knowledge was of evening gowns and symphony halls, of Prokofiev and Brahms, not Johnny Cash or Chet Atkins. The country music scene was as distant from her frame of reference as another planet.

The waitress's return temporarily interrupted their conversation. The service was set before them, glasses filled with crystalline liquid, a tray of breadsticks and fingers of cheese.

She sipped. The wine was excellent. He certainly knew his vintage. A tiny frown etched her brow as she stole a glance at him, wrestling with the paradoxes of this intriguing and disturbing man. Everything about him suggested the most irritating questions. The complications of the man were miasmic. There were depths about him that plunged to bottomless darkness. In such hidden mists and fogs could lurk specters and things that go bump in the night.

When, for example, had he first tasted anything other than wine made from blackberries picked from a thicket on a stony mountainside, or that volatile elixir known as white lightning, made in hidden stills and bootlegged to lubricate the Saturday-night square dances where he must have first played guitar? Where in heaven's name had he learned to order a delicious white Bordeaux?

And when and how had he developed a vocabulary beyond "Aw, heck" and "Y'all come?" He used words like *entourage* with casual fluency. While he still spoke with a soft drawl that had its own charm, it was devoid of the western twang and down-home phrases he used on stage. Where along the way had the ragged urchin of the coal mining hills acquired such sophistication?

He interrupted her thoughts by lifting his glass and proposing a toast. "To the Nashville experience."

"I can drink to that," she said, "on the premise that the experience in question consists of an endorsement contract signing."

"We'll get around to that, Miss Castille. By the way, do you mind if I call you Andrea?"

"Who told you that was my first name?"

"Peewee Sloan. I think you mentioned it to him sometime between your meeting at the airport and your arrival in Peewee's excellent care at the hotel."

She wondered with a sudden warming of her cheeks what other graphic descriptive rundown Peewee had offered his boss. Jess Clark had certainly shown up quickly enough after Peewee had given him a report of his passenger from the airport. Would Jess have hotfooted it to the hotel so promptly if the Castille emissary had been her grandfather? That was highly doubtful.

She might as well face the truth that Jess Clark clearly wouldn't mind mixing business and pleasure, especially where a young woman was part of the business. All of which presented her with the prospect of not returning to Tampa as quickly as she had planned, of lingering in Nashville and seeing Jess Clark more often than business demanded, a prospect that stirred an undefined and disturbing thrill quivering like a pulse beat in her slender neck. She reacted quickly to that vagrant emotion with a stiffening of her attitude.

"Andrea is the name"—she let an ice cube tinkle in her

tone—"that has the power of attorney from my grandfather authorizing me to sign the contracts."

He reacted with sudden booming laughter as if something about her was irrepressibly charming. "It's good to know you're a hundred percent legal."

She colored in unexpected embarrassment, but his infectious humor was more than catching. She wondered if anyone was wholly immune to his charisma?

She couldn't restrain a small laugh in return. But she shifted in her chair, centering herself as she stared levelly across the table at him.

"It's a legality I'd like to use at the earliest possible moment, Mr. Clark."

His humor faded. Smoke touched his eyes. There was a hint of an edge in his voice as he replied, "Yes, I believe you've plastered a hint or two on that point already."

"Sorry if I seem persistent. However—"

He ended her comment with a flick of his wrist. "No apology needed or wanted. By the way . . ."

"Yes?"

"Don't ever apologize for anything you've done that's right."

"I don't make a habit of it, Mr. Clark."

"Looking at you, I wouldn't think you did," he said with a hint of irony. Then his mood suddenly lightened again. "By the way, could you grant me one small favor?"

"Dare I ask?"

"You may. It's quite safe."

"Then what is it?"

"My name. There's more to it than 'Mister Clark.' It's Jess. Says so in the old family Bible. Right there on the page headed by births. Written there by my father a few hours after the midwife had gone home. J-e-s-s. Named for my great-grandfather, a cavalry lieutenant in the Civil War. I'd like to hear you say it.''

"This seems a little . . .''

"Ridiculous? But what is life without a few ridiculous moments? It's really very easy. All you have to do is move your lips and say it.''

"Why not?''

"Indeed. Why not?''

"Jess,'' she managed.

"As the top sergeant said to the young marine, I didn't hear you!''

"Jess.''

"Once more.''

"Jess! Jess! Jess!'' And for no reason that she could fathom, they were suddenly looking at each other across the table and smiles were tugging to a buildup of silly laughter that sent them half falling against the table. In a second the tension that had existed between them from the first moment of their meeting evaporated like a puff of smoke in the wind.

"Hey, that's pretty good, Andrea.''

"You think so?''

"Certain of it,'' he said. "Never heard the name spoken quite so nicely. Once more?''

"Really now . . .''

"Little more practice,'' he wheedled, "and we'll record it and I'll just sit around days on end listening to it.''

She tried to fight down another impulsive smile tugging at her lips and failed. She drew a breath, an awareness of herself nudging the edge of her mind. He was causing her to act like a carefree kid. *Darn you, Jess Clark, you're manipulating me. And I'm letting you!*

He was a smooth one all right. His experience had no doubt fashioned his way with women. And he certainly *had* a way with the opposite sex! She supposed women were always throwing themselves at him and he had all the strategies to fit any occasion, assessing the individual female to see which line, which approach, would work best.

The train of thought was a good, defensive reminder of the reality of the situation. Maybe he had the egotistical notion that she had chosen to take her grandfather's place because she was dying to meet the great Jess Clark. It would be just like his swollen male ego to think that! Well, she thought, no more of those girlish responses to encourage his misconception.

If he wanted to take his time to decide when he was going to discuss business, she'd just have to learn patience. But if he had the slightest notion that signing the contract would include her as another Jess Clark conquest, he could think again!

This time, she thought grimly, *your bag of campaign tricks hasn't worked.*

"Hey," he said, his eyes narrowing slightly, "you're suddenly very quiet."

"Am I?"

"Pensive." He smiled. "Must be part of the Spanish heritage."

"What is?"

"This fascinating mercurial element," he said. "This capacity to switch from mood to mood. Do you throw things when you're angry?"

"I couldn't say, Mr. Clark," she replied coldly.

"Jess," he corrected. "Depths and height. I suspect you have them in interesting measure."

She gave herself a small, secret smile. "Your assessment—I find that interesting. Mildly. However, before you place me in a neat Latin compartment, my Spanish ancestry is on my father's side. My mother was English. They met when my father was in a polo match in England."

"Very interesting combination. The dark hair and eyes from sunny, emotional Spain, the delicate skin tones from cool, stiff-upper-lip Great Britain."

She looked at him thoughtfully. "Since we are on the subject of armchair psychoanalysis, how about you, Jess Clark? You're something of a study in contrasts yourself, you know."

He looked surprised. "I am?"

"Of course. Didn't you realize it?"

"Enlighten me."

"According to what I've read and heard about you, you come from a rural background. You knew grinding poverty as a child, dropped out of school in the third grade. One would expect the kind of front you present to your audiences, a man with rough edges, down-home mannerisms, hill country speech. An uneducated man fresh out of the honky-tonks and dance halls. Yet, with me your speech and manner reflect a degree of education and sophistication that caught me totally by surprise."

The shadow of an amused smile played about his lips. "Perhaps," he suggested, "now is when I'm putting on a front. The way I appear to audiences is my natural self."

"Is that true?"

He shrugged. "Let's say that it's easy to drop all pretense and revert back to the things that come naturally."

She gave him a penetrating look. "I'm not sure what to make of you. I have the feeling that somehow you're a fraud. Either you're putting your audiences on by pretending a folksy, country-western image that's no longer the real you, or you're doing a great job of affecting a degree of urban polish to impress me."

Their eyes locked in a challenging glance like duelists touching rapiers.

"Which do you think it is?" he asked.

"I haven't made up my mind. Are you going to clear up the mystery?"

His gaze taunted her. "No," he drawled, "I reckon I'll jest set here an' let you figure it out yourself. Always keep 'em guessin', my daddy used to say."

His exaggerated reversal to his country singer role would have been amusing except for that smoky challenge in his eyes. He was taunting her in a most infuriating manner.

There was a moment of brittle silence. Then he shrugged.

"I guess just by living a lot I have acquired a little knowledge along the way since I dropped out of that little one-room country schoolhouse. Life is the best teacher. How did they used to put it? I graduated from the school of hard knocks? I like to read. I keep my eyes and ears open. Self-education, I believe it's called. You think I'm a fraud? Maybe I'm more than one person, the Jess Clark you see here and the Jess Clark people see on stage. None of us is just one person. We can be child, adult, parent, actor, depending on what the situation calls for. You came here in the role of a cool, aloof career woman. All business. But I'll bet under the right circumstances, that icy exterior could melt into molten lava, that liquid, musical voice into a throaty purr, that stiff, formal bearing into soft, yielding surrender.''

Hot, rushing blood scorched her cheeks. "I don't appreciate that kind of talk, Mr. Clark. I'm not one of your—your panting groupies! You're being downright crude!'' Angry tears blurred her vision.

Tears at what? At his insulting innuendoes? Or tears of impotent rage at herself for the way her heart hammered at his bold approach?

He bowed his head slightly. "Then I apologize, Andrea. I had no intention of insulting you.''

Meaningless words. The taunting expression in his eyes told the truth. His apology was smoke blowing in the wind. There was no escaping him or herself. Every way she turned the conversation, she ran headlong into that basic, primitive male-female attraction that smoldered between them like cinders threatening to burst into raging flames.

His expressive eyes were studying her carefully. "I sense,'' he murmured, "a withdrawal. And just when we were getting to know each other. I've offended you. I'm truly sorry.''

This time he sounded a bit more sincere. She had no alternative but to accept him at his word. After all, whatever her personal feelings, this was still the man who held the fate of Castille Guitars in his hands. She shrugged, dismissing the moment of resentment.

He went further in his apology. "I want to explain why

we can't sign the contracts immediately. I should have made all this clear in the beginning, but I assumed there was no urgency, that you wouldn't mind spending time in Nashville, do some sight-seeing, maybe even take in the Grand Ole Opry and try to figure out what's made it the longest-running performance in country music. The contracts won't be signed until my business manager gets back to town. He had to fly to Los Angeles unexpectedly. A bit of unpleasantness. It appears that a fellow out there who held a trusted position in Clark Records has been caught dipping his hand in the till.''

''Your record company?''

Jess nodded.

''I'm sorry,'' she said quietly, ''you have such a nasty problem.''

''It's not going to break me. I can get over the financial part. The rest of it . . . that will take a while to mend.''

Her dark eyes regarded him questioningly. ''By the rest of it, do you mean the betrayal?''

''Yes.'' He sighed. ''I really liked the guy. I trusted him as much as a favorite relative. Makes me wonder about my value judgment.''

A fleeting expression of sadness touched his eyes.

''What will you do to him?''

''Do?''

''I suppose you have choices.''

''Yes I do, now that you mention it,'' he said. ''I suppose I could hire someone to break both his legs in a dark alley. Or I take the legal route—prosecute and condemn him to the penitentiary. Somehow I don't find a lot of satisfaction in vengeance. 'Vengeance is mine, saith the Lord.' Besides, it would be nonproductive.''

"I'm afraid I don't follow you. He broke the law, didn't he?"

"Certainly. But if the bird is in jail, he can't very well fly some twigs back to the vandalized nest. We're going to give him the option of making restitution. He may have to sell his sports car and a house he recently acquired in Malibu, but he'll make good. He'll pay the money back and then he'll have to live with his conscience. That'll be punishment enough. Incidentally, it was that house in Malibu that finally did him in. My accountant could swallow the Porsche and his women, but there was no way the man could have bought that Malibu place on his salary." Jess chuckled wryly.

"I see," she said slowly, having just been made aware of another facet of this complex man the world knew as a simple-hearted country singer. The element of compassion in his decision was unmistakable. He was giving the man who deceived him a more humane break than he deserved.

She touched her wineglass. It was still nearly a quarter full. Moisture had beaded on the surface. She didn't raise the glass, merely sat for a moment with a carmined fingertip tracing little doodles on the wet surface. She considered this new development.

"I really don't understand," she said, "why it's necessary for your business manager to be here. All we need is your signature on the contracts. They've already been approved. Waiting for him to come back from California would only cause more unnecessary delay."

Clark's eyes took on a thoughtful expression. "Well, you see, it's not that simple."

She looked at him, frowning. "What do you mean?"

"I've had a chance to look over the negotiations since my business manager last talked with your grandfather. I'm not entirely satisfied with the proposition."

Andrea felt a dreadful sinking sensation in the pit of her stomach. After all this work, after their hopes were so high! Was Jess Clark going to back out at the last minute? Desperately, she fought down stinging tears of anger and disappointment. "Do you mean to say," she said, trying to keep her voice level, "that you've had me come all the way to Nashville believing that this deal was firm and now you're going to back out?"

"I didn't say that."

"Well, you're certainly implying it!" she exclaimed, unable to keep all of the anger out of her voice. "What do you mean, you're not entirely satisfied with the proposition?"

"Just that it's something my business manager hammered out with your people without fully briefing me on all the details. When I found out your grandfather—who turned out to be you—was coming to Nashville with the papers, I gave the whole matter closer scrutiny, and I've had second thoughts about the deal that's being offered. But it's nothing to get upset about. I'm sure it can be worked out to everyone's satisfaction."

Andrea was making a superhuman effort to keep her emotions under control. "Suppose you tell me just what it is that has to be worked out?" she demanded, her voice tight.

He tried to dismiss her concern. "Why don't we wait until Randy Davis, my business manager, gets back. Then we can all sit down and get our heads together."

"I think you owe me an explanation right here and now!" she challenged.

He shrugged. "This really is the kind of business dickering that should be handled between your company people and mine."

She was becoming more incensed by the moment. "By that I assume you're implying that because I'm a woman, I shouldn't bother my pretty, empty head about nasty ol' business matters that ought to be left up to the menfolk!"

He held up both hands in defense. "Hey . . . whoa, little lady. I didn't mean to get you so riled up."

"Mr. Clark, I'm here as my grandfather's representative with all legal powers to speak for him. I've been a part of Castille Guitars since I got out of school. I'm perfectly capable of discussing this—even negotiating, if necessary."

He shrugged, making a gesture of defeat. "I was hoping we could keep today in more of a casual, social mood. But if you insist, I'll give you my feelings on the matter. Y'see, it's not the money you're offering. I realize you're being as generous as possible. I just feel I need to be more than a hired hand, getting paid for saying a few lines on TV that some ad agency copywriter dreamed up. What it boils down to is that if I'm going to represent Castille Guitars, I want to be a part of Castille Guitars."

Andrea looked at him blankly. "I—I don't understand."

"It's really quite simple. I want to eliminate the matter of payment entirely. Instead, what I propose is a share in the ownership of Castille Guitars."

For a moment Andrea was too thunderstruck to respond. She sat stunned, feeling as if the sky had fallen in on her. "You—you can't be serious," she finally gasped.

"Sure, why not?" he said with a disarming smile. "It makes a whole lot of sense when you stop and think about it. It's to your grandfather's advantage for one thing. He doesn't have to be concerned about coming up with a whole lot of money for my endorsement. In fact, he doesn't have to pay me anything. I'll promote Castille Guitars with no charge at all."

"Well, hardly," she spluttered, "if you own part of the company!"

"But then we'll all be in this together. It so happens I do have a high regard for the instrument you people make. There's nothing finer than a Castille guitar. I'd like to see the company survive. I'd be in a better position to do that if I were an actual shareholder in the company. We'd all be in it together, sink or swim. And we'd swim, because then I'd put the whole weight of my various interests behind the company."

Andrea took several moments to compose herself. When she was able to speak, she said in a cold, level voice, "Mr. Clark, Castille guitars have been made exclusively by my family for generations. We are not a public company. We don't sell or trade stock."

"Maybe not, but right now you're about to go under. You might consider taking on a partner."

Tears of rage blurred her vision. "You're trying to take advantage of our position to take over the company! You're despicable!"

He sighed. "Trying to talk business with a woman sure is frustrating. You get so darn emotional—"

"You think *I'm* emotional?" she cried. "If you made a

proposition like this to my grandfather, he'd probably shoot you!''

Jess's face split into a lean grin that gave her a strange inner wrench despite her anger. He said, ''Then I'm sure glad I'm talking to you instead. I don't want to get shot over this!''

Then he folded his hands on the table and leaned toward her. His voice was quiet and earnest. ''Look, Andrea, I'm not trying to take advantage of the financial trouble you're having. Not at all. I'm not trying to take over Castille Guitars. I'm not even talking about an equal partnership. I just feel that if I'm really going to do you any good, I need to be directly involved with the profit-and-loss end of the business. If I spend a lot of time and effort to sell Castille guitars, then I should see my efforts rewarded by having a share in the company I'm promoting. That sounds fair, doesn't it?''

''Maybe it would if we were talking about some outfit making widgets or left-handed monkey wrenches,'' she said heatedly. ''Castille Guitars is a whole lot more than that. It's a—a tradition, a symbol. It stands for the proud name of my family. For generations it has been the instrument of great classical guitarists—''

''And,'' he interjected coldly, ''you are appalled at the thought of a crude, country-western honky-tonk musician soiling that image with his guitar-picking hands, right?''

''I—I didn't say that,'' she stammered.

''No, but you're certainly thinking it. It must be galling to your aristocratic blue blood to even be asking a hick musician like me to advertise your guitars.''

Andrea took a moment to assemble her thoughts. She toyed with a possible insight into his motivation; was it conceivable that Jess Clark's bid for part ownership of Castille Guitars had more to do with personal pride than business? Having pulled himself out of the hobo jungles, the freight yards and sleazy beer joints by his bootstraps, now he was striving for more than just public recognition? Was he looking for the touch of class that being a partner in such a proud, old-world enterprise as Castille Guitars could give him?

That could be a farfetched idea. His interest might be purely that of financial greed. She didn't know him well enough to sort that out. Whatever his motivation, it didn't matter. "It's out of the question," she said with finality.

"Look," he said, "this isn't a matter to be decided on the spur of the moment. Why don't we put it on the back burner for now. Think about it. Talk it over with your grandfather. Meanwhile, why don't we call a truce? Let's forget about business and relax while I show you around Nashville."

What other choice did she have?

As if reading her thoughts, Clark said, "Well, how about it, Andrea Castille? Since it appears we'll have a few days' wait for my manager to return, how about seeing some of Nashville? I've already suggested the Grand Ole Opry. And then there's Opryland, itself, a theme park giving you a sampling of every flavor of American popular music from New Orleans jazz to the big-band era. Altogether, the city is a tourist attraction that Walt Disney himself might have envisioned. From the entertainer's point of view it's the mecca, the place where the dreams, ambitions, hopes and despair focus. For the sightseer and vacationer, it's one of America's colorful attractions. So, how about it? Want the grand tour?"

She raised her eyes, giving him a thoughtful look. Why should she want to see the Grand Ole Opry? It would only rub salt in the wound, a living reminder of how far Castille Guitars was going to sink, forming an allegiance with that twanging, off-key music of the beer hall and truck stop crowd. The instruments bearing the proud name of Castille were made for artists of the concert stage, not honky-tonks. She should be discussing an endorsement by a performer in the classic tradition of Andrés Segovia, not the likes of Jess Clark. All the resentment she had tried to repress welled up inside and focused on the man seated across the table from her.

Then reason, like a dash of cold water, intervened, reminding her, as it had over and over on this despised trip, that she must somehow swallow this humiliation if Castille Guitars was to survive at all.

How was she going to deal with this new, unpleasant development? At the moment, it sounded like the death knell of Castille Guitars. Taking Jess Clark into the company as a partner was simply out of the question. She knew the proud, stubborn nature of her grandfather. He'd rather close the factory. Her only chance would be to talk Jess Clark out of this insane notion. But was that possible? How stubborn was he?

For the time being, she'd just have to keep her despair and anger under control and go along with this infuriating man until the problem could be resolved.

With a superhuman effort, she drew a deep breath. "If I were another tourist who just arrived in town, where should I begin my tour of Nashville?"

Chapter Three

$\mathcal{W}$ith your busy schedule, I don't see how you can find time to go sight-seeing," Andrea pointed out.

"I'm between engagements," he explained. "I'll enjoy having the chance for a refresher look at the old town. When you live in a place, you take for granted the wonderful details that give it its own personality. People who live in New York never visit the World Trade Center. Pity, isn't it? At any rate, don't worry about my schedule. I pay people to do that. So, may I plan our itinerary?"

"You're the tour guide."

"Well, we'll certainly want to take in the Grand Ole Opry. It's been the heartbeat of country music since the 1920s."

He paused to give her a thoughtful look. "I suspect you are not an aficionado of this kind of music. However, if

Castille Guitars plans to become a part of this scene, maybe you would like to learn something about it?''

''I suppose I should,'' she admitted grimly.

''Then let me give you a short course. It all started back in the early days of radio . . .''

Jess went on to tell her the story of how Nashville became the capital of the country music world.

It seems there was a Memphis newspaper reporter named George D. Hay, who made a trip to Mammoth Spring in the Ozark foothills of Arkansas to cover a story on the funeral of a World War I war hero. While there he went to a country hoedown held in a lonely cabin on a muddy back road. It was his introduction to an authentic American musical form. He carried the idea around for several years until, in 1924, he started the National Barn Dance over WLS in Chicago. The following year, he got a job as program director for a new station going into operation in Nashville, station WSM. On November 28 of that year, he started a hillbilly radio show called the *WSM Barn Dance*. On his first program, he had two entertainers, an eighty-year-old fiddler named Uncle Jimmy Thompson and his niece, Mrs. Eva Thompson Jones, who played piano. After the old-timer had been sawing away for an hour, Hays asked him if he was getting tired, and the old man had replied that a body didn't even get warmed up in an hour, adding that he'd just won an eight-day fiddling contest in Dallas!

There was nothing as fancy as a band or choral group in those early broadcasts. A few hundred country music fans way back in the boonies, straining to hear on their headsets, picked up that first broadcast on primitive battery radios and crystal sets. Nobody thought it would amount to anything. For a long time Nashville disclaimed any responsibility for the musical stepchild.

At this point in his narrative, Jess paused to ask if he was boring her with all the history.

In spite of her mingled anger and resentment, she had found herself listening with interest. "I suppose if Castille Guitars is going to be represented by one of the leading artists of your kind of music, I should learn more about it," she said, trying to sound civil.

"I get the distinct impression it's not your kind of music." He smiled.

"No, frankly, it's not. I don't mean to sound like a music snob, but my musical tastes lie in other directions. However, I would like to learn how this kind of music became so popular. Please go on."

"You used the word *popular*. You put your finger on the heart of the matter. Once, when I didn't have anything better to do, I looked up the definition of the word *popular* in the dictionary—'Of or pertaining to the common people or the whole body of the people. Beloved or approved by the people.' I especially liked that last line, 'Beloved or approved by the people.' That, to me, is what popular music is and what country music has become. It's the poetry of the people, the stories of everyday life set to music."

Andrea listened thoughtfully, aware of his intense feelings about his music and trying to grasp his meaning. It wasn't easy for her. Their backgrounds were too different. Still, she found the conversation intriguing. "Go on," she encouraged.

"Okay." Jess returned to the history of the broadcasts.

"Amateur performers started coming out of the hills on mules and Model T Fords, bringing their harmonicas, Jew's harps, fiddles and washboards. There was David Harrison Macon, better known as 'Uncle Dave Macon,' also called the 'Dixie Dew-Drop,' the 'king of the banjo pickers,' the 'Squire of Readyville.' Uncle Dave charmed audiences with his humor. His collection of rural songs went back to the 1800s. His skill with the banjo was outstanding. He joined the Opry in 1925 and was a star performer for fifteen years until he died. Other early performers were Humphrey Bate and his daughter, Alcyone, the Crook Brothers and Kirk McGee. But the singing group that had the greatest impact on the world of hillbilly music was the Carter family, Alvin Pleasant Carter, his wife, Sarah Dougherty Carter and his sister-in-law, Maybelle Addington Carter. Maybelle's daughter, June, is now married to Johnny Cash.

"One night in the late twenties, when the show followed the NBC classical musical broadcast moderated by Walter Damrosch, George opened the *WSM Barn Dance* by saying, "For the past hour you've been listening to Grand Opera. Now we will present grand ole opry!" That name stuck. The Opry outgrew a lot of its barns in the years that followed. First it was held in the WSM studios, then a tabernacle, a theater, the WAR Memorial Auditorium. From 1941 to 1974, it was held in the Ryman Auditorium. Today the Opry House is a big, modern auditorium located in Opryland."

Jess explained that over the years the music evolved and changed, branched in different directions: bluegrass, western swing, rockabilly, the Nashville sound. Eventually there developed a difference of opinion between the traditionalists and the innovators as to the authenticity of country music. The traditionalists believe that pure country music instrumentation should consist of only fiddle, guitar, mandolin, string bass and five-string banjo. No amplified instruments and definitely no brass or reeds— just straight, unadulterated bluegrass instrumentation. For years the Grand Ole Opry fought against the rhythm instruments of the western swing bands.

Jess grinned. ''D'you know, the first time a band used a set of drums in a Grand Ole Opry performance, they had to hide the drums behind the curtain to keep the group from being chased off the stage?''

They both laughed. Once again, Andrea felt the companionship they had shared earlier. In spite of her resentment of the kind of music Jess Clark represented, she was intrigued by his story. She thought his promised tour of the city might not be so bad.

''These days,'' Jess said, ''when performers bring their hopes to Nashville, they come to the right place. Nashville is where it's at—Music City, U.S.A. New York and Hollywood have been moved over to second fiddle in the great string band of golden pop. Tin Pan Alley did all right in its time, but these days it's the music industry here in Nashville, Tennessee, that's playing the cash register rag. More than half of all recorded music in the U.S. originates in taping sessions in Nashville's recording studios. It's become a multimillion-dollar-a-year business.''

Yes, Andrea was all too well aware of the commercial

success of the music business in this city. That's why she had come here hoping to save her family's business.

She rose. "Well, shall we get started?"

"I'm ready, unless you'd like to change or freshen up first?"

"Not unless I look inappropriate. I chose the outfit for traveling comfort."

"You look perfect," he said, his lingering gaze taking in much more than just her outer garments.

Again, she felt that unwanted quickening of her pulse.

He said, "I think we should start our jaunt from the top of the Life and Casualty Tower. It's the high rise practically within hollering distance. From the observation deck we can see Nashville, the river, the fields and woods. It's a vantage point from which I can point out quite a number of locations. After that orientation, we'll be on our way. We'll save things like the Grand Ole Opry and the Country Music Hall of Fame for tomorrow. But today you might enjoy visiting an example of a true antebellum plantation mansion, Belle Meade."

There seemed no way she could escape his taking her arm. His car was brought from the parking garage. It was, as she expected, a jaunty sports model. He opened her door with a flourish. As he helped her in, his hand brushed the curve of her breast, igniting a throbbing flash of heat. Had it been an accident? Flustered, she settled in the curve of the bucket seat.

His gaze swept over her again, lingering for a moment as she arranged her skirt over her long legs.

"Comfortable?" he asked.

No, she wasn't. Not with him looking at her that way.

Not with her pulse racing and her breast still aching from the brush of his hand. But she managed to say evenly, "Yes, quite comfortable. Let's get started."

The early evening sky was a softening twilight in the east and a dying crimson glory in the west when they returned to the hotel.

They paused in the lobby.

"Jess, thank you for a lovely day." Had she uttered those words? she asked herself with wonder. Surprisingly, the experience had turned into one of those special times she would long remember.

He had been every bit the gentleman. As a self-appointed tour guide he'd offered sidelights on the passing scene that brought landmarks alive and awoke the city's rich heritage of history. When he steered the conversation in a more personal direction, it had been aimed courteously at drawing her out; he asked where she'd lived as a child, how she'd become involved in her grandfather's guitar business, little sidelights extracted by his genuine interest. He'd made her feel appreciated as a three-dimensional person. He had lulled her into feeling relaxed with him. He could be a charming and witty companion.

But then there were those times when a certain glance would put her back on guard—glances that stirred within her a wild, crazy certainty that nothing was hidden. Those eyes could focus through the details and expand an intimacy to which he had no right. They could drift over her and make her feel as if her garments had been shed, one by one, even as they strolled, not touching, through Belle Meade mansion and their voices discussed a portrait or a hutch or an armoire. They could—oh, damn those eyes!—nudge her toward the unwilling, shocking and most unexpected primitive fantasies. She remembered the moment when passing through a bedroom in the mansion, a canopied four-poster bed had suggested the intimacy of rumpled sheets on a warm, moon-filled summer night perfumed with Confederate jasmine, and a woman with a thickly beating heart stretching in lazy-kitten sensuality as she reached to welcome the male presence passing through the moon-glow to her awaiting bed.

She'd ripped her eyes away and moved quickly from that room! Perversely, aggravatingly, frighteningly, she'd had the suffocating feeling that if she didn't get out of that room, the X-rated fantasy would zoom in on the figure on the softly perfumed bed and she would see herself. And beside the bed would hover the eyes ablaze with passion in that craggy face, and moonlight would glint on the wiry curls on the broad chest, and the powerful arms corded with muscles hardened by the earlier years of manual toil would reach to touch her. . . .

He'd had to move quickly, there at Belle Meade, to catch up with her in the corridor outside the bedroom. The eyes had glinted in soft, lazy amusement. "Quite a bed in there. No wonder they had so many children!"

Her cheeks burning, she had desperately changed the subject. "I wonder whose portrait that is, the stern old gentleman looking down on the gallery. . . ."

Belle Meade. The high point of their afternoon journey. One could easily imagine the gracious balls and dinners given there after this queen of Tennessee antebellum mansions was built in 1853, the strolls in honeysuckle-scented moonlight, the high-spirited thoroughbreds foaled in its stables, cavorting coltishly in the soft green of its pastures. Belle Meade, still here in the twentieth century, with the preserved elegance of its furnishing and appointments, testimony to a Nashville that treasured every aspect of its culture.

Now, in this glittering hotel lobby resplendent with its own contemporary elegance, Jess was also remembering those magic moments at Belle Meade. "At Belle Meade," he was saying, "in those surroundings, I heard the first chord whispered like a diminished seventh with a passing melody note lurking off the edges."

Her gaze was riveted on his face. She sensed being in the presence of some kind of invisible, undefined movement.

"After Belle Meade," he explained, "a melody kept murmuring in the background, trying to clarify itself. And when you spoke about the lives lived so long ago in that setting, the couples who must have laughed and played and made love, you gave me the theme of the lyric, I think."

"You mean," she said in mild amazement, "these last few hours you've been writing one of those fabulous Jess Clark songs?"

He made an apologetic gesture with his broad, strong hands. "Sorry, can't help myself. It just happens. Never know where the process will originate or what triggers it. Sometimes it aggravates the hell out of me, like when I wake up in a small hour of morning and can't do anything but lie there with my head full of words, melodies and harmonies that just haven't quite come together. But get one thing straight—being with you was the song today."

She was flustered, caught unawares, flattered and shaken. "If—if you experienced one of those creative moments, I'm glad,'' she said. "After all, it's your profession, your career. But I doubt that I was the inspiration.''

"Don't be too sure.''

Those eyes again, searching, probing relentlessly, searing depths that should have been her private domain. She wiped her damp palms nervously on her skirt, then held out a hand in what she hoped would appear as an impersonal gesture of friendship. "Well, thank you again. And I suppose I'll see you tomorrow?''

"Tomorrow?'' His eyebrows were raised in genuine surprise. "But how about tonight?''

"Tonight?'' She looked puzzled.

"Yes, the party at the Quackendalls.''

She shook her head, bewildered. "I'm afraid I don't understand.''

Now it was his turn to look puzzled. "It was made clear in our message to your grandfather. A special Nashville-style barbecue cookout had been planned in his honor. Since you are representing him I naturally assumed . . .''

She felt genuinely embarrassed. "He didn't say anything about it. I—I suppose in the last-minute rush of getting me off it slipped his mind. He's growing a bit forgetful, the old dear. And so many business worries have been on his mind lately.''

"Well, no matter. Now that you know, you'll come, won't you? People have been invited. A lot of preparations have been made. You have plenty of time to get ready.''

"Yes, I—I suppose so, under the circumstances. Who did you say was giving the party?''

"The Quackendalls, part of my team, Hooter and Marilee. Hooter is my drummer, best in the business.

Marilee, his wife, is something of an authority on hill country folk songs. They have a lovely place on the river. I'll pick you up at seven-thirty. That okay?''

She glanced at her watch. ''Yes. Then I'd better hurry up to my room.''

In her room, she went directly to the telephone and placed a call to Tampa. Her grandfather responded quickly. She gave the preliminaries in a nutshell. The flight had been fine. She gave him her room number. More important than anything else, how was he feeling?

''I'm fine,'' the old man said impatiently, ''just as I was when you left early today.''

That was not entirely reassuring. He'd looked tired and gray, his eyes reflecting a weariness he'd refused to admit to when he'd bid her good-bye this morning. Now she heard the same weariness in his voice. *''Mi abuelo,* nothing is important if you're not—''

''Dios!'' the old guitar maker exclaimed. ''If you were someone I'd hired as a nurse, I'd fire you within five minutes, Andrea! You'd probably whip out a thermometer every time I blinked!''

She smiled, her concern easing a bit. At least the Latin temper could still throw sparks.

''Now get to the point,'' he said. ''I assume you have met Jess Clark and had a first conference with him?''

''Yes.''

More than just a conference, she thought, her whole body growing warmer.

''And he's signed the papers?''

The pleasant afterglow of the hours spent with Jess faded with a jolt. For the past few hours she had been living some kind of dream fantasy that had filled her emotions with golden clouds, obscuring rational thought. But now, suddenly, the cold reality of Jess Clark's unreasonable demands returned, jarring her back to reality. What kind of spell had he cast over her to make her temporarily forget the threat he had become to her and her family?

A chill made her shudder at the thought of telling her grandfather about Jess Clark's new conditions for promoting Castille guitars. A partnership in the company, no less!

It was simply impossible to break that kind of news to her grandfather over the telephone. He would have apoplexy on the spot. No, she had to play for time, hoping against hope that somehow she could persuade Jess to relent and accept the original terms.

How she dreaded having to disappoint her beloved grandfather! ''Abuelo,'' she stammered, ''He—he hasn't signed the papers. Not yet.''

There was a muffled expletive in Spanish. ''And just when is this elusive signature going to be visible on the contract?''

''His—his business manager is out of town,'' she said lamely.

''What has that got to do with it? We need the signature of Jess Clark, not his business manager!''

''I know, Abuelo, but it's the way he does business. He refuses to sign anything until his business manager is here.''

''And when is this phantom business manager going to materialize?''

"I can't say exactly. The business manager had to go to Los Angeles on an urgent matter dealing with the Clark record company."

She could picture the way the old man was holding the phone, slender hand tight, knuckles whitening. "Do you think he's just stalling, playing a game with us?"

She swallowed hard. She had never lied to her grandfather before. It wasn't easy now. "I—I don't think that's it."

"No more aces up his sleeve? No more double-talk? Andrea, after all the long negotiations we've been through! We've offered the best we can. He has got to realize that."

"Well . . . it's just this matter of the business manager not being here. Clark seems to refuse to make a move without the man."

There was a pause. "Andrea, are you telling me everything? You sound strange."

"Do I? Well, it's all the excitement, I suppose. The flight here—you know how I hate flying. . . ."

To her relief her feeble excuse seemed to convince him. "Well, my dear," he said with a note of resignation, "I suppose we've no choice but to await the pleasure of the country music virtuoso. Meanwhile, we'll maintain a positive attitude."

"Of course, Abuelo."

"One final suggestion. While you're there, mix a little enjoyment with this annoying business. See a few of the sights, dine at a special place or two, catch a live performance. I understand there's much to see in Nashville."

A secret smile tugged at her lips. "Yes, Abuelo, I've

already done some sight-seeing. Oh, by the way, had you been invited to a cookout party this evening?''

''Oh, yes!'' She could hear him slap his forehead. ''I completely forgot to tell you. I knew something had slipped my mind in the last moments' distractions. Yes, the matter of a cookout did come up. I suppose that's the sort of thing those people there do.''

Andrea felt a surge of relief. Then tonight's party wasn't something Jess had dreamed up on the spur of the moment, a superficial ploy to claim her company for the evening as part of his male conquest.

''Since all the arrangements have been made, I suppose I should go as your proxy.''

''Yes, I don't see why not, if you don't mind. There should be young people there. You'll enjoy yourself, probably more than I would. Have a good time, Andrea. Leave the problems of Tampa in Tampa. Raymond Ayers is on top of things here. He's a good factory manager.''

Yes, she thought, in his quiet, efficient way, Raymond Ayers is doing the best that could be done with what was left of Castille Guitars. But even a managerial genius couldn't conjure up customers.

''Speaking of Raymond, he said if you called, to give you his love,'' her grandfather added.

The thought of Raymond, of the people in the old loft and of the smells of glue and freshly painted wood gave her a momentary homesick twist of the heart.

''Give Raymond my best,'' she replied.

''I will. He cares a great deal about you, Andrea,'' said her grandfather. ''When you come back with the contracts, we'll all celebrate. Now you go on and have a good time tonight.''

"You, too. Don't spend the whole evening at the shop. Go home, put your feet up. Watch some television."

"All right." The old guitar maker chuckled. "Bye, Andrea." He hesitated. Then he said softly, "I love you, my little Andrea."

She lowered the phone slowly into its cradle and sat looking at it for a moment. "I love you, my little Andrea." Something in the way he'd said the words gave her an uneasy premonition, as if he'd wanted to give the words a special meaning because he might not be saying them much longer.

She put the thought out of her mind. She had enough to worry about tonight, facing an evening together with Jess Clark. The more she was around him, the more she feared she was facing problems of the heart rather than those involving Castille Guitars.

Chapter Four

The hissing of the warm shower on her bathing cap and the softly curving litheness of her body was relaxing. She squeezed soap from her rag over her shoulders and turned around and around, letting small rivers of soapy warmth trickle over her bosom and down her back. Then she increased the pressure, relishing the sensuous massage of the steaming shower all over her body.

She turned the temperature to cold, dancing in the chilly deluge. Out of the shower, bundled in a comfortable terry-cloth robe with a turbaned towel replacing the plastic cap that had covered her hair, she felt languid. It occurred to her how busy the day had been. It seemed ages since she'd watched Tampa recede, the early sun glinting on the lazily friendly Gulf thousands of feet below, then vanish as the jetliner had pierced cottony cumulus, a silver javelin aimed at the heavens.

The subject of Jess Clark was an insistent mental preoccupation while she went about the routine of getting dressed. He had been as fresh when they'd returned to the hotel after the sight-seeing journey as when they'd left. She wondered what it would take to dull his vigor, to sap the stalwart body that suggested tough, hewn oak. Apparently he had never faltered, flagged or succumbed to fatigue in the onslaught of a schedule that must be horrendous—the jumps between one-night concert appearances before thousands of adulating fans, the twice or thrice nightly shows when he performed in locations like Vegas or Tahoe, a conference in New York in the morning and a recording session in Nashville in the afternoon with perhaps a club appearance that night.

She sat at her dressing table, lazily brushing glistening black hair that hung down her back to her waist. She paused in the rhythmic stroking to gaze off into space, lost in reverie.

Never in her life had she met a man like Jess Clark. He certainly did not fit the mold of Mr. Average. She made an effort to sort out her feelings about him and only became confused. She remembered that she had started out being wary of him, nervous about the unwanted, primitive emotions he stirred, angry with herself for having feelings that made her so uncomfortable. She had known very little about him other than the image of masculine charisma that he projected with such devastating impact. Somewhere along the way, this afternoon, he had begun to emerge as a person. While remaining wary of him—and of her own feelings—she had discovered things about him that were quite human and admirable.

Perhaps it had started with the discovery of his humane treatment of the record company executive in California. He had shown a side that surprised her. He was apparently vulnerable to being deeply hurt by betrayal at the hands of someone he trusted yet able to turn the other cheek. He had a marvelous sense of humor. At times he relaxed and let the little boy in him take over, becoming mischievous and lighthearted. Maybe it was that touch of the child in all creative artists that made them so appealing. Yet, with it, there was the other side of him that was mature and responsible. She had to respect what apparently were deep, sincere religious convictions that made his gospel songs convincing.

Then how could he be such a rascal with women? She was baffled by the conflicting complexity of the man. She sensed a streak of nobility in him, but running in counterpoint was the element of a prowling jungle cat—an earthy masculine predator. She thought she'd trust him with her money but certainly not with her heart! On that ground, she remained wary.

The problem was that she was beginning to like him and that was dangerous. She felt safer when they were adversaries.

A glance at her watch brought her out of her reverie with a start. Quickly she finished with her hair, catching it up in a gold barrette near her right ear so that it cascaded richly over the front of her shoulder. It resulted in an exotic but carefree effect, far different from the severe, no-nonsense bun she had worn earlier.

Before showering she had taken out her light travel iron and quickly pressed a hint of luggage wrinkle from a pair of navy-blue Corbin slacks and an Evan Picone blouse. She was glad she had brought along a pair of strappy sandals to coordinate with the casual outfit that seemed appropriate for the evening's festivities.

In fashion she favored the tailored, traditional look, good anytime, anyplace. She thought it smart economy to shop for quality garments. She wasn't a closet stuffer. She liked quality clothing because it fit properly and looked good time and time again, proving more economical in the long run.

Dressed now, she stepped back from the full-length closet door mirror for a quick, final inspection.

The mirrored image might have been chosen by a photographer to model the clothes. Its attractiveness was enhanced by the naturalness of supple movement as she turned this way or that as she looked at herself objectively. It seemed unusually important to look right this evening. She felt that the glamorous hairstyle complemented her designer outfit, giving her an overall look of casual elegance.

Her thoughts persisted in focusing on Jess Clark and the evening ahead. This catch of breath, this soft tremor of butterfly wings in the stomach—how really ridiculous. She was acting like a young teenager with a pulsing heart trying not to peep out the front window so she could rush upstairs and have to be called by a parent on the arrival of her first date.

For heaven's sake, Andrea, come off it! What's this silliness? What's gotten into you?

The evening ahead was certainly not a tryst in some romantic cafe in Casablanca! It was no more than a friendly cookout, of all things, to which she was going as a proxy replacement for her grandfather.

She grew calmer thinking of it that way. She could admit to herself that, yes, Jess Clark's charisma included the threat of fascination. She could further admit a response to his presence, an enhancement that had made the tour of Nashville today a bit more than just routine sight-seeing. She had found herself not wanting the day to end. But that hardly meant she was in a total state of enchantment, a sorcerer's helpless captive until a rescuing power appeared to perform an exorcism!

The phone rang. It was Jess calling from the lobby. Should he come up to her room to escort her to his car? She glanced around at the intimacy of the hotel room and reacted with panic. No, she told him hurriedly. Wait for her in the lobby; meet her at the elevator. She would be down at once. She hung up before he could debate the matter.

She stepped coolly from the elevator, offering the neutrality of a casual smile as she moved out into his presence. That dark, brooding gaze swept over her, glinting with an expression of surprised approval that warmed her from head to foot. "What a transformation," he said, unable to take his eyes from her. "I thought you were a beautiful lady the minute I laid eyes on you this afternoon. But you were in the role of a young business-woman, dressed and looking the part. Now you've turned into a glamorous, ravishing movie star. Must be the way you're wearing your hair. . . ."

His voice trailed off. He appeared unable to move, again oblivious of everything except her.

She felt her cheeks grow uncomfortably warm. "Please, Jess. For heaven's sake—you're embarrassing me."

A slow smile curved his lips. "I'm the envy of every man who looks at us," he murmured.

"And I of the women," she exclaimed. What harm in returning an innocuous compliment?

Indeed, even if he were not a celebrity, Jess Clark would draw the eyes of every woman in the lobby. His more-than-six-foot frame handsomely filled a gray suit designed with a western cut. The bronze of his face was emphasized by a white shirt. He wore a western-style black string tie, and of course the usual custom-made, hand-crafted western boots. She thought he must have a closet full of them and they must be worth a fortune.

With an air of old-world gallantry, he escorted her from the air-conditioned lobby into the humid warmth of the southern night. Part of his charm, she thought, must lie in his ability to make a woman feel utterly feminine around him. Men who were successful with women seemed to have that talent. In his case it came quite naturally. There was nothing affected about it.

An attendant, as if standing by on instruction, was parking a snooty two-seater with its cloth top down. The car rated a second glance even from a disinterested party. She guessed it was a beautifully restored Mercedes of vintage age.

The attendant sprang out, came around and held the opened passenger-side door for her. The glove-leather upholstery was inviting beneath her slender weight as she sank into the seat.

Jess handed the youth a tip, walked around and got in

beside her. Deftly, he swung the car from the curb into the flow of slow inner-city traffic.

"Fresh air okay?"

"Oh, yes." She tied a scarf around her hair, enjoying the caress of the warm breeze.

She watched the passing hustle of a vigorous and self-confident city. The people in the morass of cars and on the sidewalks all seemed to be going to someplace where they wanted to be.

She was increasingly relaxed in the comfort of the seat. Must be contagious, she thought, this air of well-being in the midst of passing strangers.

She let her head rest contentedly against the top of the seat and slipped a covert glance at his profile. The wind stirred that determinedly errant lock of hair across the chiseled height of his forehead. The styling of the dark-brown, coarse, heavy mane was mussed about his ears. That didn't detract from his looks. In fact it made his profile almost brutally attractive.

In the wan reflection of light from the instrument panel and the rise and fall of brilliance from the streetlights they sped past, his hands on the wheel were broad and strong, with finely curled black hair. His build, his movements even in the way he handled the car, made her think of a feline animal, a panther that roamed the mountain wilderness of his native state.

She realized with a start how closely she was examining him. She cut her gaze away, taking refuge in casual conversation. "I really enjoyed the sight-seeing trip today. As you said, Nashville is a fascinating city."

"Oh, we didn't even scratch the surface today," he protested. "Tomorrow, perhaps, we can go to the Parthenon with its statuary and painting. Then we can see the Country Music Hall of Fame. I think you'd enjoy the Country Music Wax Museum. The figures of the immortals of country music look so lifelike you're sure any minute they're going to step right out and say hello. In the afternoon we'll take a riverboat cruise on the *Captain Ann*. Then you'll think you've stepped back into the era of Mark Twain and the early banjo pickers. After that, we could make some of the Music Row attractions—the Music Row Mall, Music Row Entertainment Center, Country Corner USA. We'll need tickets for the performance in the Tennessee Performing Arts Center to hear Mr. Jack Daniel's Original Silver Cornet Band playing a concert with our American heritage as its theme. For relaxation in the evening hours we can spend some time on Printer's Alley, and visit clubs where we'll hear great musicians like Boots Randolph. All that will give you an introductory handshake with Nashville. You'll begin to catch the little details of the people and places that make up the flavor of the only town that could produce the Nashville sound.''

"Heavens!" she exclaimed. "I'm exhausted before I begin. Surely we couldn't do all that in one day?"

He gave her one of his lean grins. That mischievous glint in his eye that was so fatally charming caught her breath in her throat. "You're right," he drawled. "Might take two or even three days. I'm in no hurry, are you?"

She was dangerously close to confessing that, indeed, she wouldn't mind at all stretching out the time she was spending with him. She thought it safer to change the subject. "Tell me something about the people giving the cookout tonight."

"The Quackendalls?"

"Yes. What did you say their first names were, Hooter and Marilee?"

"Correct."

"Where did he ever get a name like Hooter? It's a nickname, I presume."

Jess laughed. "As near as we can figure out, it's his real name. His daddy gave it to him because he came into the world hootin' and hollerin'. At least that's what Hooter claims. The family lived so far back in the North Carolina Smokies there weren't even moonshiners. Hooter says the only way his daddy could shut up his hollering was to play the fiddle while Hooter wriggled and kicked the sides of his crib to the rhythm of the music. By the time he was toddling, he was banging on a saucepan and shaking pebbles in a tin can every time the fiddle started sawing away. He was hardly out of the diaper stage when his daddy made his first little drum like the Cherokees do it, stretching rawhide over the ends of a small hollowed-out log. Hooter has been beating drums ever since. Today he's the best in the business for my money."

"And his wife, Marilee? Does she play in your group, too?"

"Yes. That little lady plays fiddle like they're going to take it away from her any minute." Jess laughed. "She and Hooter are the most unlikely couple you'll ever meet. Reminds me of that old saying about marriage making strange bedfellows. Her background is as remote from Hooter's as the moon. Marilee comes from an old Boston family. She was educated at Vassar."

"How on earth did they ever get together?"

"Must have been fate. Ever since high school Marilee

was interested in folk music as an art form, a grass roots expression of the common people. It started out as a hobby, but by the time she was of college age the interest had turned into a passion and became her life's work. She spent her summers in Appalachia researching the art form, tracing its history, defining it. She lugged her tape recorder all over the Carolina hills, hiking to some remote cabin if she heard there was an ancient old-timer living there who could sing a song his grandfather had taught him. She's written two definitive works on the subject, standard references for colleges that include folk art in their curriculum.

"Somehow in her trips around the Appalachian countryside, her and Hooter's paths crossed. They've been inseparable ever since. They're a very devoted couple. If I ever fired one, I'd surely lose the other. Not that I have any intention of doing it."

The scene was changing outside the car. They had left the urban scene behind. They passed occasional houses separated by green fields and patches of woodland. A rural dirt road intersected the two-lane asphalt state road they were on. A country store complex offering general merchandise, eats and a service station flicked by them at the intersection.

"Hmm," Andrea murmured thoughtfully. "I met Peewee Sloan, your keyboard man. Hooter is your percussionist and Marilee plays fiddle. Who else is in your group?"

"The baby is Skeeter Kelly. Skeeter plays electric bass and doubles on tenor saxophone. He was a mere nineteen years old on his last birthday. Skeeter's folks had their hearts set on seeing him in Vanderbilt, one of the fine universities in Nashville. But Skeeter's never had anything in his head but music. He just squeaked through high school, not for lack of brains but because he spent so much time hanging around musicians. Skeeter used to help an old mechanic in a rundown garage get a brake job out of the way so there would be time for a few tunes. The old guy was a whiz on the chromatic harmonica. He taught Skeeter refinements in improvisations when the beat is hoedown and the chords are coming fast. On Saturdays, Skeeter would hang out at flea markets where the local pickers would drift together for a pass-the-hat performance. The boy soaked it all up like a sponge. His idol is Boots Randolph, one of the truly great saxophonists of all time. Skeeter spent his allowance on tickets for all the Boots Randolph performances. If Boots played out of town somewhere, Skeeter would scrounge bus fare or hitchhike. I guess it all paid off. Skeeter is what we call a natural. He was born with an excellent ear and sense of harmony. He took a few music lessons in high school but in six months he was playing rings around his teacher!''

''It appears you have a colorful and highly talented group,'' Andrea observed.

''You'd better believe it. What we do is more than one individual or even the sum total of the parts. If I can explain . . . Well, sometimes even the best musicians do it mechanically as a group. Then on rare occasions you get a chemistry: it works; it grooves; it goes. Know what I'm saying? These people, their improvised counterpoints and accents, their phrasing and subtle tonal qualities, they show off Jess Clark as nearly to perfection as he'll ever be. I'm indebted to all of them.''

There was a humble quality to his statement that

surprised her. In a reflective mood, she watched the passing country scenery. She had thought of country music as a primitive cacophony of musical illiterates, an insult to the classical reputation of Castille Guitars. She had resented this entire unpleasant business of having her family's reputation as fine instrument makers represented by a country-western singer. But admittedly, she hadn't known much about the idiom until she'd encountered Jess Clark. His dedication to his kind of music impressed her.

There was a glow of pride in his voice as he talked about his group. "My people are the cream of what we call sidemen. They don't need me for bread. Such people are in constant demand by the studios as artists for recording sessions. Everybody's looking for good arrangers and writers. The Nashville-based Broadcast Music Incorporated, known in the music business as BMI, licenses most of the country-folk-western songs for performances commercially throughout the world, returning royalties to the composers." He laughed. "Would you believe that Skeeter, at nineteen, is now earning a lot more money than his father makes? Skeeter gets regular royalty checks through BMI, having already coauthored two songs recorded by artists in the Glen Campbell class."

"Do you sing them?"

"You bet I do and darn glad to get the chance." He shrugged. "I know I'm good. Maybe I'm very good. I know it when I hear the playback of a number I did right. I also know that I'm not as good as I'd like to be and intend to be. And I know what my people do for me and what I do for them."

She felt hushed, her psychic processes tentatively feeling through darkened doorways, sorting out, making assessments. The world of Jess Clark was becoming ever more real, making her aware one moment of a frigid blast, the next of a warm glow. It was a world wherein the very talented succeeded if they were lucky and found themselves rich, sought after, cajoled. But it was also a world of dog-eat-dog. The closer the player got to the top, the sharper the fangs of the snapping jaws.

Jess had also cracked the door open an inch wider on himself—the man, not the image. She wasn't sure how she felt about that. The more she knew, the more she was aware of obscure, bewildering, unsettling depths—depths that fascinated, frightened and at the same time lured an insidious compulsion to explore areas that caused the fantasies.

What if—she felt herself stir languorously—what if Jess, that roughshod survivor, took over, the corded arms ensnaring her, the chiseled lips smothering her protests, the hands seeking, touching, demanding, the fire of him crackling through her, overwhelming her? . . .

"Did you say something?" he asked.

She realized she'd dismissed the unwanted fantasy with a stricken little gasp. "Say something? Oh, no. Maybe I made a murmur at the countryside. It's so beautiful."

"Yes, and it will be even more so in a little while. There'll be a full moon tonight."

Oh, no, she thought. Even nature was conspiring against her this evening.

He slowed the car and turned onto a side road of white gravel. It looked like a private driveway but no house was visible. The white ribbon wended its way into a stretch of woods that paralleled the highway.

He stopped the car after driving a few yards. The

headlights revealed a broad gate between two stone pillars. The pillars anchored a fencing of high wire in either direction.

Leaving the engine at idle, he opened his door. She watched him walk to the gate, taking a small plastic key from his wallet. He slipped the credit-card-sized key into the steel casing mounted like a mailbox on the right side of the stone pillar. She watched the gate swing open, obeying coded electronic impulses. She knew the device would sensor the car's passage and close and secure the gate after them. The same security device would also flash signals to the house somewhere ahead as well as to the nearest police command post if the gate or fence were improperly breached.

He slipped the key back into his wallet as he returned to the car.

The snowy gravel crunched softly as the car rolled slowly forward.

"Is it a big place?" Andrea leaned slightly forward, trying to pick out details in the darkness.

"Covers about three hundred acres. Hooter likes to have room, he says, to throw something if he feels like it, without hitting a neighbor."

As they followed the course of the driveway through the woods, Andrea saw the rise of the land up ahead to a low ridge. The long knoll was silhouetted in a fan of light from a source hidden by the slope.

They slipped from the shadows of the trees, crossed a green, mown meadow, and when they crested the low hill she saw that the light came from mercury vapor lamps on tall stanchions set about a hundred feet apart.

The pool of artificially created private daylight was

roughly the size of a football field. It bathed a rambling, low-roofed ranch-style house that appeared to be made of redwood, wrought iron and glass. The driveway forked near the house, one branch curling in front of the home and expanding in a parking area where several cars sat. The other fork veered off toward the dark hulking out-buildings, a barn, stables, pastureland demarcated by split-rail fencing. The furthest building might have escaped Andrea's notice had it not been for a tall, stainless-steel pole rising from a shallow gable. A silvery wind sock drooped at the top of the pole in the evening stillness, suggesting a hangar for a small airplane—a Cessna, perhaps.

The bright area revealed life: one person crossing from the house to a large swimming pool, another busy in the area of a barbecue grill, a third appearing near the end of the house to wave a signal of welcome to the approaching headlights of Jess's car.

He chose a vacancy in the parking area between a station wagon and a dusty Chevy van. As they got out, Andrea caught the enticing aroma of steaks broiling on a hickory fire.

A welcoming committee of one approached them. She was a petite young woman with flaming red hair and a sprinkling of cinnamon freckles across a pert, turned-up nose. Her blue eyes sparkled. "Hi, Andrea. I'm Marilee. Jess phoned us about the change of representatives from Castille Guitars. Wish your grandfather could be here, too. Welcome to our home, which is yours also as long as you're in this neck of the woods."

Andrea liked her immediately. It was obvious that Marilee was an open, warmhearted person who never knew a stranger. She put Andrea at ease and made her feel completely welcome. If she was indeed from Boston, a graduate of Vassar as Jess had said, it was not apparent from her speech. Apparently she had become so immersed in country music lore and its music makers that it was reflected even in her soft drawl.

Marilee linked her arm through Andrea's as they strolled the flagstone walkway toward the picnic area. She glanced around at Jess, who was on the other side of Andrea. "And you only said she was beautiful! You're losing your lyrical touch, Jess."

His laugh was pleasant. "I've been searching for words to do Andrea justice the whole afternoon."

Marilee's pat on Andrea's shoulder was sisterly. "Hope you're good and hungry."

"Umm. Those steaks have my mouth watering."

They rounded the corner of the house and there was the massive Peewee, half-drained beer mug in his right hand, spreading his big arms for a friendly bear hug of welcome. "Andrea, has this guitar picker been showing you a proper good time?"

"I must admit that he has." She felt bubbly, her cheeks glowing in the contagious good humor. She was getting the impression that Jess's group wasn't run of the mill. In an environment where there was often much vanity and displays of arrogance and backbiting by egocentric personalities, it appeared that Jess had attracted a group of very special individuals.

"Andrea," Peewee said sententiously, "if he doesn't treat you right, I'll be pleased to break his nose for you."

"I doubt if it would hurt any worse the second time," Jess said pleasantly.

Andrea glanced at the tall man beside her. For the first time she noticed the curve at the bridge of the thin, hewn nose. It was true; at one time Jess's nose had been broken. She wondered what the circumstances had been. A railroad dick throwing him off a freight train, guitar, duffel bag and all? A beer bottle thrown during a brawl in some dive where his voice had first been heard? Accident in a coal mine?

Another voice cut into her thoughts. "Howdy, Andrea, ma'am."

The owner of the voice had strolled over from the cooking area to greet her. A white apron and tall chef's hat looked somewhat ludicrous on his tall, rawboned frame. He had the reddish complexion that went with sandy hair. His bony body, homeliness and the awkward way he moved made her think at once of Abraham Lincoln. He smiled shyly and gravely shook Andrea's hand.

"I'm Hooter," he explained, as if it were necessary. No one else there could possibly be named Hooter. And meeting him now, she couldn't imagine him having any other name.

By now they'd all moved onto the patio near the swimming pool. A redwood table covered with white linen was laden with appetizers and salads. An ice carving of a swan floated in a punch bowl filled with frosty red liquid. There was a choice of cocktail or highball mixings and nearby sat a large oaken beer keg.

"Cocktails before dinner?" Jess suggested.

"The punch bowl looks inviting," Andrea said.

"Hooter's own recipe."

"I named it Scarlett O'Hara," Hooter said modestly. "It's easy and simple to make, mostly cranberry juice blended with citrus and given a little character with Southern Comfort.''

"A lot of character," Jess warned. He filled a crystal-line punch cup and passed it to Andrea, then dipped one for himself. Andrea sipped and found the drink delicious but potent.

"Hi, there."

She turned to greet the new voice. He'd approached from the parking area, a fair-haired boyish figure in jeans and a black T-shirt across the chest of which white stenciled letters asked the question, "Have You Sung a Song Today?"

In the angles of the lean, peach-fuzzed face, his eyes were a sparkling blue, his smile wide and spontaneous. He had to be the precocious youngster of the group, Skeeter Kelly. Despite his youth, he was as tall as Jess and had the same look of graceful power and energy in his move-ments.

"Hello. I'm Andrea. You must be Skeeter."

He wiped his palm on his jeans and shook her hand. "Pleased to meet you, ma'am. Hooter, where's the grub? Can't you see the lady here's starved?"

"He's speaking about his own chronic condition." Marilee laughed. "Skeeter could eat his way through a deli and have a candy store for dessert."

"I'm still a growing boy," Skeeter protested, reaching for a handful of hors d'oeuvres.

"Come and get it!" Hooter called, lifting a barbecue cover and releasing a waft of hickory smoke. Duckling, ribs, saddle of beef, all oozing sizzling juices sat on the grill.

The entire group filled country-kitchen-sized plates and there was a sudden lull in the banter. Before she had taken three bites, Andrea decided Hooter could give the chef at the Waldorf a few tips. The lazy minutes built a sense of relaxed repletion and Hooter's coffee in steaming mugs was the perfect topper.

"Anybody feel like a swim?" Skeeter suggested.

Marilee added, "We have extra swimsuits, Andrea."

"Maybe a little later. Right now I'm too stuffed to move!"

Skeeter ambled off in the direction of a low-roofed bathhouse with four doorways facing the pool. He opened a door and stepped into one of the dressing cubicles.

Hooter seasoned the talk courteously in the direction of Andrea's interests. The conversation touched on her life in Tampa and her family's guitar factory.

In the company of these people, Andrea found herself talking candidly about her life. Then she became aware of the way Jess, sitting on the bench beside her, was listening, head turned slightly sideways, the dark eyes unmoving as if catching every movement of her lips, every nuance of expression flitting across her face.

She became very self-conscious. Her voice hesitated in the midst of a humorous anecdote about the conniving tricks of a New York importer who shipped scarce, fine-quality German spruce so important to the manufacture of Castille guitars.

"If he ever goes out of business," she finished lamely, wishing Jess's brooding gaze would shift to some other direction, "I suppose Raymond will have to climb a Bavarian mountain and cut the wood himself."

Jess stirred. "Raymond? Would that be your factory manager, Raymond Ayers, the fellow who has been involved in our negotiations?"

"Yes, that's the Raymond."

"What's he like?"

Something in his voice made it seem like more than an idle question. Andrea was thinking how to answer when everyone's attention was distracted.

"Hooter, you traitor, you've been cooking in my absence!"

The musical feminine voice belonged to a pixielike blond gamin entering the circle of light.

Andrea sensed a stiffness in Marilee's movements as she rose to greet the newcomer.

"Hello, Nori."

Chapter Five

Jess and Hooter had risen also, dropping napkins on the table.

Nori paused a few feet away, her eyes sweeping the scene. She stood on slightly spread feet, hands on her hips, arms akimbo. The stance smacked of challenge, accusation and anger mingled with hurt at being the uninvited.

Skeeter stepped out of the bathhouse, wearing swimming trunks. He tossed a casual wave and a "Hi" at Nori as he moved to the deep end of the pool.

"Well, I see it's the same familiar troupe," Nori said. "Is there a drink reserved for me?"

"Sure," Hooter said. "Ain't there always?"

Nori ignored him. She seemed to be ignoring everyone but Andrea. She came a step nearer the table. The brightness of the lighting wasn't wholly kind to the elfin image. Andrea suspected that the girl was certainly no older than the early twenties, essentially a cuddly, lovable blonde. But she had faded early and the freshness was absent due to the drawn look about the edges of her small face. She wore makeup to smooth the faint wrinkles at the corners of her blue eyes, which were fastened on Andrea's face. In their depths Andrea detected lurking anxieties and an element of hostility.

Why? Andrea wondered. They were total strangers. Why the expression of dislike in Nori's eyes?

Andrea's first swift impression of a sweet young girl emerging from the shadows shifted to that of a woman who perhaps had seen too much of life in too few years. And not during a routine nine-to-five life-style by any means.

"Nori, this is Andrea Castille," Marilee introduced her. "Andrea, Nori Lawrence."

"Oh, yeah," Nori said. She ignored Andrea's proffered hand, reaching instead for a glass and a bottle of Scotch. "Guitars."

"Yes." Andrea nodded, not knowing what to make of the girl's attitude.

"You sure as heck don't look like an old Spanish don come here to nail down Jess's name for your guitars!" Nori, with apparent carelessness, splashed a full three inches of straight whiskey in her glass.

"My grandfather was unable to make the trip. I came instead to finalize the signing of the contracts." Andrea tried to sound pleasant despite the girl's coolness toward her. The young woman was making her feel ill at ease for no apparent reason.

"Can't say that I blame you." Nori gave Jess a thin

smile. She came around the table and raised her hand to rest it possessively on Jess's broad shoulder. "Why don't you let the master here show you around Nashville during your stay? He knows every nook and cranny." Nori lifted her glass and took most of the Paul Bunyan-sized drink in one grimacing gulp.

With a stir of embarrassment for another person, Andrea realized Nori was drunk. Quite drunk. In fact, she was bombed. She had obviously driven out here alone, arriving by the grace of some miracle that had kept her from killing herself or someone else on the road. Apparently she was one of those people who can walk straight, talk without slurring and keep their eyes from crossing right up to the point of supersaturation, after which the final straw seems to break the camel's back all at once.

Andrea thought, with a mixture of pity and dismay for the young woman, that it took a lot of practice to play the game that way. It looked as if Nori'd had ample practice.

The explosion of the Scotch triggered the inevitable chain reaction to Nori's overloaded nervous system. Andrea could almost see herself flickering out of focus in Nori's eyes, feel the sudden sickening lurch in Nori's brain as the scene tilted.

Her small, sweet mouth turned down at the corners. She lifted the glass unsteadily to kill the drink, trying to think of what it was that she had wanted to say.

Jess's hand clamped over her slender wrist.

"Don't you think you've had enough, Nori?"

"Leave me alone," Nori said petulantly, trying to shake loose. "You got a lotta nerve, leavin' me waitin'!"

"Come on, I think you need to take a little nap."

Jess gently took the glass from her numbed fingers, put it on the table, encircled her with his arm and led her toward the house. She walked in stumbling steps, her head resting against Jess's broad shoulder.

Marilee watched them go. She muttered, "After forty winks, that kid'll bounce up like a chipmunk, bright-eyed and bushy-tailed, ready for another go at the old track record."

Andrea's gaze followed Jess and the girl as he led her to the house. Her mind and emotions were in a state of confusion. She felt an inner cold draft. What role did Nori play in Jess's life? What was the nature of their relationship? She had touched him in the possessive manner of a woman who has a certain claim on a man. And he was treating her with a caring, concerned gentleness that didn't go along with casual friendship.

"What did she mean by Jess's leaving her waiting?" Andrea asked impulsively. Had he left the little blonde cooling her heels while he squired the brunette stranger from Tampa around the marvelous old town? If that were the case, then Jess was a rat and she could understand, if not condone, Nori's drunken behavior.

"Don't pay no attention to Nori." Hooter shrugged. "She just wanted to start a scene."

He got busy with the chores of cleaning up the remains of the meal. Marilee slipped her arm through Andrea's and they strolled to the pool, settling in deck chairs. "Have you ever heard the name Nori Lawrence before, Andrea?"

"No."

"Well, I suppose some country folk music fans

haven't, either, but they're a minority." Marilee idly watched Skeeter frolicking in the water like an overgrown Labrador retriever. "Nori, 'the Skyrocket' Lawrence." Marilee sighed. "I guess that's a good way to describe Nori, considering how skyrockets go up like they're headed for the moon only to fizzle out and fall back to earth, empty and spent. Y'know, the trade papers and DJs called her that when she was on the way up: 'The Sunny-Haired Skyrocket.'

"Maybe it came too early and too easy for Nori," Marilee went on, shaking her head. "We all have to pay our dues. Nori never realized she got her ticket on the roller coaster at a bargain price. She didn't knock on Music Row doors until her knuckles were raw. She hadn't been around long before a young assistant executive arranged an audition. And she was in. Her first single was cut with a vocal backup, Billy Joe and the Firecrackers. After only two exciting, starry years in the business, Nori had a gold record. There was talk in the business of a nomination for a country music award. Nori was in way over her young head, going at a killing pace. She was living in a millionaire's condo, driving a Bentley, wearing originals from Paris, flying New York caterers down for fabulous parties. She let herself fall prey to that retinue of freeloaders and blood-sucking yes-people who crowd around a star. Like the old saying goes, she was living in a house of cards. When the winds changed, she was left on a foundation of quicksand. The adoring hangers-on melted away. The fans started applauding someone else. She hadn't saved a dime, of course."

"What happened?"

"The public is fickle. This kind of success is like a wisp

of smoke. Her life-style robbed her performance of the fresh, young spontaneity that had charmed the fans. She started missing performances, leaving crowds in the lurch. A couple of records bombed. That's about all it takes to end a career.''

Andrea was touched by the brief summation of a short human life. She was touched by pity as well as a shiver of fright. Music City could be so generous—and so cruel. Now Nori had nothing left, Andrea thought, except a few loyal friends like Hooter, Marilee, Peewee and Skeeter. And Jess? Andrea couldn't escape the implications of Nori's air of possessiveness. What was included in the untold subplot of Nori's story?

There was a moment of silence. Andrea struggled with a nagging question that she finally found impossible not to ask. ''Are she and Jess good friends?''

Marilee shrugged, looking in another direction. ''They've known each other a long time.''

It was an evasive answer. Marilee obviously did not want to be put on the spot. Was she covering up for Jess? That was a likely possibility. This group was as close knit as a family.

The evening for Andrea had become troubled. This new development of Nori Lawrence had stirred a maelstrom of feelings that she really didn't want to examine too closely. She had been caught off guard by the whole thing. She had especially been caught off guard by her own reaction.

She stared at the swimming pool. It beckoned, inviting hard, physical exertion as a refuge from her disturbed feelings. ''You mentioned a swimsuit I could borrow?''

''Sure. Most people are squeamish about wearing a used bathing suit. I know I am. So we keep a supply of new bathing suits on hand in case a guest shows up unprepared. Please pick any one you want and take it home with you when you're through. You'll find everything you need in the bathhouse.''

Andrea was impressed by the thoughtful hospitality. It was nice to be affluent enough to treat guests so royally.

A few minutes later, Andrea emerged from the dressing room in a red bikini that revealed a long-legged, curvaceous figure. She had removed her barrette and now her black hair flowed down her bare back.

Jess was nowhere to be seen. Andrea glanced at the house. The sumptuous, sprawling structure offered no clue, but she knew he was still in there . . . at Nori's side.

She cast it aside with a toss of her head, walked to the end of the diving board and entered the water in a beautiful racing dive.

Skeeter was treading water close enough to splash a few drops in her face when she surfaced.

"How about a race?" he challenged.

"Sure," she agreed, shaking the water from her eyes and pushing strands of hair back with both hands.

"Okay, but anyone who dives like you do has got to give a handicap. I get a quarter length head start in a four-lap race. How about it? Betcha fifty cents."

She laughed. "I think I'm being conned, but okay. I won't mind taking your money!"

She wasn't surprised to find that Skeeter was very good. On the second push-off, glimpsing the shower of bubbles in his wake, she estimated that she had cut in half his handicapped start. She might need more than four laps to beat him.

Gritting her teeth, she stretched a little further and

quickened the beat without losing the coordination necessary to the fullest efficiency of her smooth Australian crawl. Third push-off. By veering she could have grabbed his ankle. On the final lap he was still a body-length ahead.

She tapped all her reserve energy for the final sprint and they burst upright at the end of the pool in the same instant, each reaching for the supportive edge of the pale-blue tile while they laughed breathlessly and flicked a finger of water at each other.

"I guess we'll have to match for the half-dollar, Skeeter." She gasped, sucking breath into her starved lungs.

"Fair enough," Skeeter agreed, his breathing slowly returning to normal. "Ready for another glass of Hooter's punch?"

"No, thanks."

"Guess I'll have another snack. All this exercise makes me hungry." He swam to the nearest ladder, then splashed wet footprints on the way back to the picnic table.

Andrea surface dived and drifted aimlessly underwater, just letting the freedom of her weightlessness and the softness of the water massage the tensions from her long, supple muscles. Rising to the surface, she writhed onto her back, floating, kicking her feet just enough to keep them buoyant. Then she turned over and down again to touch the bottom of the pool.

At home she often played in the water like this. Sometimes she would sing some silly ditty while floating on her back in the sweeping expanses of the bay. On one occasion, she had felt a shadow, jerked her head and there had been a sailing dinghy almost beside her, drawn to explore the source of the throaty female voice singing "Mairzy Doats." A ruddy-faced old retiree with funny gray side whiskers had peered over the side of the little boat. "My stars," he'd exclaimed, "I think I found a mermaid."

Embarrassed, Andrea had headed for shore. The little sail of the dinghy had bobbed in her wake all the way back to the Castille dock. Then, before sailing off, the friendly old man had lifted his rumpled yachting cap, exposing a totally bald head, and bowed. "Thanks, young lady," he'd called, "for making an old man's day."

Suddenly the image of the elderly gentleman dissolved into a much younger image poised on the diving board watching her with the kind of male hunger the old man in the dinghy held only in sighful memory.

This image—Jess Clark—was a broad-shouldered package of slightly rawboned sinew balancing its six-feet-tall hundred and seventy-five pounds on corded legs. His skin was tanned deeply enough to lighten the shadow of body hair on his arms and legs, the curly brush moving in the rhythmic rise and fall of his deep chest.

Jess certainly had the physique to model his tan swimming trunks.

A warmth suddenly engulfed her. He'd said nothing, was merely standing remote and stiff as a statue, watching her. She knew he'd come out, had seen her in the pool and changed quickly while she was playing at being a happy dolphin.

She looked around almost desperately. Hooter, Marilee, Peewee and Skeeter had drifted up to the house. They were out of sight, out of hearing range. She was totally alone with this man who seemed enrapt by the refracted images of her that he saw in the shimmering water.

She swallowed hard. Treading water, she backed slowly away from the diving board. She drew a breath that became caught and entangled in the pulse beginning to beat wildly in her throat.

"Hi. How's Nori?"

"She's asleep. She'll be all right when she wakes up. Mind if I join you?"

"It isn't my private pool."

His dive wasn't bad, a movement of raw power without subtle refinements.

She swam lazily away as he bobbed up, and again he followed. She let her feet drift to the smoothness of the ceramic tile bottom and stood in waist-deep water. He reared beside her, showering water with a shake of his head. Droplets clung to his lashes, making them look longer, sootier—shadowy framing for the dark depths of his eyes.

"As you can see," he admitted, "I'm a dog-paddler from an old quarry pond."

"I imagine you'd get across the river all right. Maybe much better than some of those with the nice, smooth movements taught by an expensive coach."

"I watched you dive and race Skeeter. You're very good," he said.

"Thank you," she murmured, trying to keep her voice light in denial of the way his eyes were burning over her, seeming to see through her bikini. The water suddenly felt like a silken caress on her tingly skin.

"Perhaps you could give me some lessons," he said softly.

"Sorry. I'm not qualified as a swimming coach."

He swam a few strokes, stopped and turned to face her again, standing in chest-deep water.

She stood there with her heart beating wildly, acutely conscious of their bodies clothed in the barest minimum of garments.

He was drifting closer.

Stand back, she thought desperately.

His face was close to hers.

And she realized dimly that it wasn't he who had moved. He had stood perfectly still; only his magnetic force reached out, drawing her blindly closer to him.

His eyes held her in a powerful grip as his hands slid seductively up her bare, wet arms, sending a shudder through her body. Only inches separated them. She could almost feel the heat of his body radiating through the water to her. Breathing became difficult. His eyes with their dark, swirling depths steadily gazed into hers on a journey of exploration that sapped the strength from her knees.

"Jess," she whispered in a strained, almost pleading tone. "No. . . ."

But his hands slid up to her shoulders, then to her back, pulling her toward him, removing those last inches of separation. Her bare thighs touched his, and fire licked through her nerve ends.

She knew with a certainty that carried a special element of panic that he was about to kiss her.

"No, Jess," she repeated, this time with more conviction. "This is total insanity. We only met a few hours ago."

He nodded. "Yes, I know. It happens that way some times, doesn't it? Chemistry or something between a man and woman. I think I wanted to kiss you that first minute I saw you in the hotel lobby. You felt the same."   "No, I didn't!"

"Maybe you wouldn't admit it to yourself."

"Don't be ridiculous," she retorted, raising her chin. "I don't go around wanting to kiss strangers."

"Do you think of me as a stranger?"

"Well, yes. You certainly were a stranger when we met this morning in the hotel lobby. I still don't know much about you."

"Do you have to know everything there is to know about another person to feel attraction? Maybe a certain amount of mystery adds to the appeal."

"It also adds to the insanity!" she said, wishing she could put some distance between them.

She tried to draw away, but he was gently sliding his palms over her slippery back in a way that turned her resistance into a mockery.

His lips were slightly parted. She could catch the gleam of strong, square teeth, the moistness of his tongue as it touched the curve of his chiseled lips. "You know a whole lot about me," he pointed out. "You've read all the publicity releases, the story of my life in a dozen magazine articles."

But that told her nothing about who the real Jess Clark was. And how about Nori? What part did she play in his life?

That was only one of a dozen questions swirling

through her mind like sentences written on scraps of paper spinning in a whirlwind. In her present state of mind, she couldn't hold on to any rational thought. Reason was drowned in a rush of emotion and sensation. His hands were sliding lower on her back, pulling her closer. Her body, feeling utterly naked, was molded to his, melting in the heat of the contact.

Some dim voice of self-preservation, all but drowned in the throbbing pleasure of the moment, reminded her how easy it was to go beyond the point of no return. The only safety factor was in not getting into a situation like this. She should never have gone for this swim!

Damn you, Jess Clark, she thought with an inner whimper, where did you learn to caress a woman like this? His hands sought every secret curve and hollow with a gentle, exploring touch that was both delicious and hypnotic. She could only stand helplessly, like a captured doe, gripped in a hypnotic spell she could not break.

His mouth found hers and she responded with an abandoned hunger that shook her to the depths of her being. Never had a man's kiss aroused such a fierce, primitive response! For this insane moment, all restraints were thrown aside. Nothing mattered except hungrily tasting the burning intimacy of his lips and teeth and tongue.

His arms had become iron bands around her, and hers responded with a strength of their own, rising to wrap around him, fingers curling, nails digging into his back.

The bottom of the pool seemed to fall away. They drifted below the surface, locked together. A quake of fright went through her. Perversely, the fright itself became a delicious ingredient in the fatal precipice toward which she was plummeting. Her arms and legs were entwined with Jess, their bodies locked in a feverish embrace.

Drowning was the least of her worries, but eventually, lungs straining, they drifted to the surface.

Then, the startling shock in the form of a woman's voice returned them to reality.

"Jess."

Andrea pushed away from Jess and swung around. There on the edge of the pool, fists thrust in jacket pockets, stood a white-faced Nori Lawrence. Her eyes were no longer fogged and vacant. They were bright, glassy, filled with—what? Andrea tried to interpret the range of emotions churning in the young woman's gaze, but found them too violent, too complex to identify.

Chapter Six

$\mathcal{B}$ack in her hotel room, Andrea dropped her purse in a chair and paced restlessly, hugging her arms as if trying to keep her inner being from flying apart.

This day had played havoc with her. She felt drained, emotionally and physically.

Pausing before the large windows, she stared out at the lights of Nashville. When she'd boarded the plane in Tampa early this morning, she had never in her wildest imagination anticipated that such turmoil would be awaiting her in this city. Jess Clark had, in the few short hours she had been there, taken her reasonably well ordered, rational life and turned it into emotional confetti.

The drama replayed itself in her mind from start to finish, refusing to relinquish her from its powerful emotional grip. She remembered clearly the start of it, the curious effect of that publicity photograph of Jess Clark that she had gazed at on the plane and then the devastating impact of meeting the man himself. Never before had she felt such overpowering attraction. She had fought it bitterly, losing ground each moment she was around him. ''Chemistry,'' he had called it. Perhaps it was something in his body, an electromagnetic force that made contact with a force inside her that had been lying dormant since the day she was born. He had unleashed that force and now it was consuming her.

Damn him, for this power to nudge, twist, turn her . . . making her absolutely schizoid, one part wanting to become one with that clean, piney-woods masculine scent of him, the other wishing desperately that she were safely back in Tampa, taking a deep breath of gratitude for getting safely out of this crazy place.

Yes, in a sense it was the place as much as the man. In her feverish state of mental agitation, Jess and Nashville seemed to merge into one. He was the city come alive in one person. He represented Nashville and Nashville was Jess Clark. The two were inseparable. The city's conflicting rhythmic beat of success, glamour, romance contrasted with its earthy underside of smoke-filled honky-tonks and barroom brawls. It was a perfect reflection of Jess's life.

The memory of that kiss in the swimming pool flooded through her, setting her body afire all over again and turning her cheeks red with shame. She found it hard to believe the wanton, abandoned woman who had surrendered so avidly to Jess Clark's embrace was really Andrea Castille. Maybe she really was schizoid! Could she be two persons inside one body? She stared at the mirror and saw the reflection of a cool, poised young woman of aristocratic bearing. But lurking behind that icy façade was a woman who could be aroused to the most fundamental primitive passions by a man whom she hardly knew.

It was insanity!

Infatuation. Pure and simple, romantic infatuation, the kind that turned adolescents into mooning idiots. That was the only sensible way to describe the state she was in. It had nothing to do with love. She wasn't even sure she liked Jess Clark.

He could be charming and amusing and devilishly attractive. He was polite and courteous in a kind of courtly, old-fashioned way that would flatter any woman and cause her to melt inside. But those were his company manners, not uncommon in a man raised in the rural southern backwoods tradition, where men were taught to treat women with a certain amount of chivalry.

What was the real Jess Clark like? He had demonstrated that he could be ruthless with a woman. Tonight in that savage embrace in the swimming pool when his kiss had unleashed an explosion of primitive emotion, he had shown that he had no regard for her as a person. He had said nothing about love or even caring about her. He had been bluntly truthful. "I wanted to kiss you that first minute I saw you in the hotel lobby," he had said. His commitment went no further than that. As far as he was concerned, he was after a headlong rush to make a conquest, to claim her and satisfy his male ego, which was hungry for a woman who had aroused his desire.

Should she feel flattered that a man so attractive and sought after would find her so desirable? Perhaps. Maybe that partly explained her response to him. It should also warn her that she was playing with emotional dynamite that could only tear her own life apart.

Then she thought about Nori Lawrence, that missing part in the jigsaw puzzle of Jess Clark. After they'd left the pool and had gotten dressed, Jess had told her, "I think I'd better drive Nori home, Andrea. In the state she's in, she's sure to start drinking again. She'll insist on driving and she might wind up killing herself or somebody else. She gets stubborn as a mule when she's like this. I'm the only one who can do anything with her. Would you mind if I ask Peewee to see you back to your hotel?"

"No, I don't mind."

"We're still on for tomorrow's continuation of our sight-seeing trip, though, right?"

"I—I guess so," Andrea had replied uncomfortably, wondering how she could get out of it.

"I'll call you first thing in the morning," Jess had promised.

Andrea felt a curious mingling of relief and some other very disturbing emotion. She could identify the relief clearly enough. After that kiss in the pool, there'd have been no telling how the evening would have ended if Jess had taken her back to the hotel. She was downright afraid of being alone with Jess anymore tonight, though not as afraid of him as of herself! She gave a silent prayer of thanks to whatever guardian angel had delivered her from Jess Clark into the big, safe paws of Peewee Sloan. But what was the other dark emotion running counter to that feeling of relief? Could it be jealousy of a little blond fallen angel who obviously had some claim on the life and heart of Jess Clark? Why did these mental images of Jess driving home with Nori's cuddly body snuggled close to him keep flashing in her mind, causing a sickening lurch in her stomach? Why did she have to picture Jess carrying Nori in to her bed, her arms tightening about his neck, their lips meeting, Jess comforting and reassuring her that she was his woman and Andrea was no more than a passing fling?

Jealousy? Andrea shuddered with a fresh wave of humiliation. Really now! Could she be that adolescent?

If not, then why was she so disturbed by that comment Nori had made, demanding of Jess, "Why did you leave me waitin'?"

Jess's friends had brushed Andrea's questioning aside. But surely it could mean only one thing: the hurt, angry accusation of a girl who had been stood up by her man. Somewhere in today's chaotic events, Jess had left Nori cooling her heels while he went chasing after the dark-eyed stranger from Tampa.

If true, that did not say a whole lot for Jess's morals.

It also awoke in Andrea the dark suspicion that Jess was going after her to make a conquest, figuring that Andrea's body was an unspoken part of the deal in his signing the endorsement contract with Castille Guitars.

A sudden, blinding fury exploded in her brain. Was it possible that Jess Clark put that meaning on her trip here in place of her grandfather? Could he believe that Castille Guitars was so desperate and Andrea so conniving and immoral as to offer herself to sweeten the deal?

She wouldn't even put it past the rat to have invented the story about his business manager being out of town, just to give him more time to score with her!

"Oh!" she gasped. With pent-up fury seeking release,

she snatched a pillow from the bed and hurled it at the suitcase that contained Jess's photographs and press releases. If her suspicion were true, she wished the picture were Jess in person and the pillow a concrete block!

Andrea stormed around the room, caught up in a rampage of anger and humiliation.

Then, somewhat exhausted, she collapsed on the bed, staring wide-eyed at the ceiling. Her thoughts grew calmer and more rational. She made an effort to assess the situation from a standpoint of logic. Viewing her actions and feelings objectively, she could see her response to Jess as no more than a case of infatuation. Perhaps somewhat juvenile, but within the boundaries of normalcy. Coming to that conclusion, she was able to stop castigating herself so much.

As for Jess Clark, the kindest assessment she could arrive at was that he was simply an attractive male animal on the prowl. The worst, that he viewed her as an added bonus to the financial arrangements between himself and Castille Guitars.

With all that laid out, where did she stand? Well, she thought, she had little choice. She couldn't pack up and go running back to Tampa. Too much was at stake. Until Jess's signature was on those contracts, she had to go on playing the game, being cordial to him, maybe even flirting a bit until she could cajole him out of his impossible demands of a partnership in Castille Guitars.

It would be dangerous, but she would do it. And once she pulled it off, she would grab the first plane back to Tampa!

Feeling somewhat better about the situation, Andrea spent the next half hour washing the chlorine from her hair and taking another shower. Then she turned out the lights and settled down for the night.

She was just falling into a restless sleep when the telephone sounded, jerking her from her pillow.

With shaking fingers, Andrea fumbled for the bedside light. Again the telephone rang, its genteel buzzing magnified a thousand times with its threatening implications jarring her taut senses. She stared at it as if it were a snake about to strike.

Who could be calling but Jess? Why would he be calling?

The telephone rang for the third time, demanding a response. With cold fingers, she reached for the instrument. ''Yes?''

''Andrea?''

She recognized the voice at once. It wasn't Jess. It was Raymond Ayers!

''Raymond!'' she gasped. ''Are you here in Nashville?''

''No, Andrea. I'm in Tampa. . . .''

She started to tremble. A black mist clouded her senses. She fumbled for the boudoir chair beside the phone table for support. ''What's wrong, Raymond?'' She was surprised at the steadiness of her voice. Somehow, in the first instant of hearing Raymond's voice, she'd felt and accepted the nature of what was wrong. ''It's Grandfather, isn't it?''

''I'm afraid so, Andrea.''

She struggled to make her vocal chords function. ''Is—is he . . .''

''No. I wish I could tell you more about his condition, Andrea. We have him in the hospital in intensive care.

They haven't had time to run all the tests and tell me much yet.''

But he was alive. She grasped at that straw. ''What happened, Raymond?''

''Well, I had dinner with him at his home. We talked about the usual things, problems at the factory, your trip. After dinner we went into the library for his usual after-dinner coffee and cigar. Suddenly he clutched at his chest, gasped and collapsed. I immediately called EMS and a squad responded promptly. I'm sure he's going to make it. But at this stage in his life and circumstances and his state of health lately—well, my first thought was to call you.''

''Yes, of course. You did the right thing. I'll see if I can get on a red-eye flight back to Tampa immediately.''

''All right. I'll check schedules and be at the airport when you step off the plane.''

She hung up and for a moment stared at the instrument, too stunned to move. Like a sleepwalker coming awake, she shook her head and looked around the room. No need to pack anything, she thought. If necessary the hotel could package her personal contents and ship them. Until she found out how serious things were back home, she'd keep the room.

She picked up the phone. ''Get me the airport, please,'' she told the desk clerk.

Chapter Seven

The misty gray dawn enveloped her when she disembarked in Tampa. The air felt heavy, oily, as if it were a salty exudation from a becalmed Gulf of Mexico that had turned into a Dead Sea.

The dismal humidity did nothing positive for Andrea's sagging spirits. She felt tangle-haired, travel-rumpled, gritty-eyed as she walked through the mists that made weird halos about floodlights and runway markers.

She didn't see Raymond Ayers right away and the absence of his familiar figure was a dim and distant disappointment. It made her realize how much she'd been counting on the sight of a friendly face.

Then she saw him, pushing through a cluster of people with a lack of propriety that wasn't Raymond's usual style.

He was beside her, his troubled eyes searching hers in a sympathetic perusal. They embraced and he kissed her.

"Raymond, is he still alive?" were the first words that leaped from her lips.

He nodded reassuringly. "Very much so, Andrea. In fact, things seem to look better this morning. I just came from the hospital. They're still getting test results, but they're beginning to give the impression that things aren't as bad as we first thought."

"Thank God," Andrea said prayerfully.

Then he took her bag, his other hand a steadying grip on her elbow as they walked through the glaring lighted areas inside the terminal. "The doctor should be at the hospital when we arrive and he can tell you more about the situation."

About them, the unique life of the airport continued, oblivious to her own private drama. Flights were being announced; travelers were lined up to receive luggage; people were having coffee and early breakfast in the restaurant; luggage handlers were scurrying; a chic flight attendant who'd overslept rushed past on tapping heels, hurrying to make her schedule, flight bag bouncing on her shoulder strap.

Now a glance at Raymond's face made her realize guiltily that he was about as pooped as she was. It had been a long night for him, too. His full face, usually glowing with health, was drawn and tinged with gray.

He was not quite as tall as Jess Clark and wasn't as lean. There was very little resemblance between the two men. But that didn't mean that Raymond was nondescript. In his three-piece business suit, white shirt and coordinated

necktie, he had the look of a young executive on his way to
the leather chair at the head of the executive board table.
The fact that he'd worn the clothing since yesterday and a
faint stubble shadowed his jaw did not detract from the
image.

His face didn't have that wolfishness hinted in the lines
of Jess Clark's. It was a bit softer and more genteel. His
nose had certainly never been broken by a flying beer
bottle in a barroom brawl!

His eyes were gray, reflecting quick intelligence. His
hair was fine, in soft waves of auburn that glinted when
the light caught it at a certain angle. One day his body
would probably flesh out to portliness and gray would
brush his temples, giving him that distinguished look
some men in the boardrooms strive for and struggle to
keep in health clubs.

Raymond would never have massive crowds screaming
for him during a concert. He wouldn't mark his successes
with gold records on a wall or his name in the columns of
national gossip magazines. He might never be known
outside a small circle of people living sane, predictable
lives. But he was nonetheless important. The complexities
of modern society couldn't function very long without the
Raymonds.

The thoughts had tapped the deep-seated depths of her
friendship and respect for Raymond and Andrea linked her
arm warmly with his as they crossed the parking lot to his
car, a sensible small navy-blue Buick.

The Florida sun was a fiery splash of crimson in the
east. By the time the Buick had reached Bayshore Boule-
vard, the sun was a bright-silver orb casting rays across a

breathtaking inverted blue bowl of sky, lancing shards that danced in the rippling waves of Hillsborough Bay.

Raymond slowed and smoothly turned onto the short causeway connecting the mainland to Davis Island. Soon they were pulling into the parking area of the multistoried Municipal Hospital.

Andrea and Raymond made their way to a large desk to face a pleasant middle-aged woman in the uniform of a hospital volunteer. Andrea identified herself and asked about her grandfather. The woman flipped through a rotating file. "Yes, dear. He's still in intensive care. I doubt if they'll let him have visitors."

"Can you tell me anything about his condition?"

"Well, you'd have to ask his doctor about that."

Andrea gave Raymond a questioning look. "Dr. Racklin, Andrea," Raymond said.

She nodded. Of course, Gene Racklin had been her grandfather's physician for some time. She felt reassured, knowing he had an excellent reputation as one of the city's top internists. "Is Dr. Racklin in the hospital?"

The woman behind the desk glanced at a board containing a list of physicians' names. Small lights were on beside some of the names. "Yes, he's in the building. He's probably making rounds. You might go up to the third floor and ask at the nurse's station."

She and Raymond stepped out of the elevator and walked toward a cluster of nurses.

"We're in luck," Raymond exclaimed. "Look."

Andrea recognized the figure of her grandfather's physician. They approached him quickly, Andrea's heels making quick tapping sounds on the polished hall floor.

"Dr. Racklin!"

He glanced up from a clipboard he was studying, the earpieces of a stethoscope dangling out of the side pocket of his white medical jacket.

"Well, Andrea, hello. And good morning again, Raymond. Guess it was after midnight when we last parted company."

"My grandfather, Dr. Racklin. How is he?" Andrea demanded anxiously.

"The results of the tests are coming in, Andrea, and right now I'd say things are looking better and better."

"Oh, I'm so relieved to hear that," she said tearfully. "Was it a heart attack?"

"Tell you what. Let's find a quiet place to talk." He turned to the nurse in the station. "Could you please give me the chart for Manola Castille?"

The nurse turned a large, rotating file, pulled out a metal-bound chart book and handed it to the doctor.

"Thanks. Come along, Andrea. Oh, Raymond, you can come, too."

"I think it may be better for Andrea to talk with you alone," Raymond said. "I'll just wait out here."

Andrea shot him a look of gratitude for his understanding. The doctor escorted her into a small conference room. She sank into a chair. Racklin perched himself on the edge of a desk, silent for a moment as he scanned the chart.

"Yes, your grandfather had a heart attack, Andrea. But it looks as if it was a mild one. We're keeping him in intensive care right now because he's still having some arrhythmia—irregular heartbeat. But we can control that.

We have some excellent drugs these days to treat heart conditions, medicines that weren't available a few years ago.

"It doesn't appear that much damage has been done. He should have a good recovery. But it's going to take more than pills to keep him well. He's going to have to make some changes in his life-style. For one thing, he's going to have to give up those strong cigars he somehow gets smuggled in from Cuba. More than that, he needs to get out from under so many business worries. This first attack was something of a warning. A second one could be a lot more serious, maybe fatal."

"I know he's been under a lot of strain lately," Andrea said. "I've been worried about him for weeks. The business has been going through a crisis. To my grandfather, the guitar factory is his life."

"Stress." Dr. Racklin nodded. "That's today's killer all right, responsible for the epidemic of the twentieth century, high blood pressure, arteriosclerosis, all the medical problems your grandfather has. This first attack was a warning that his system is breaking under the strain."

"Would a bypass operation help?"

"I don't think it's gotten to that point, yet. I'd rather treat him with medicine and see how we do. He needs to stop worrying so much. Do you think his business may turn around any time soon?"

"Possibly. Raymond came up with the idea of launching a promotional campaign, tying one of the top country music stars with Castille guitars. His name is Jess Clark. Maybe you've heard of him?"

"Oh, sure. I've seen him on a number of television specials. He's one of the biggest stars in popular music these days, isn't he?"

"Yes. All the aspiring young country singers and musicians want to emulate him. Raymond thinks if they see television spots with Jess Clark playing and promoting Castille guitars, they'll want one of the instruments. It could open a whole new market for us. Until now, Castille guitars were only known in classical circles."

"Well, that sounds like a smart move. Raymond is a sharp businessman. Let's hope it succeeds. I'd like to see your grandfather get out from under so much pressure." He closed the chart.

Andrea rose from her chair. "Can I see him now?"

"Probably better if you wait a little. We have him pretty heavily sedated. I think it would be wise if you wait until this afternoon, after lunch. We'll have him out of the IC unit then and in a private room. He'll be waking up and able to talk to you. Meanwhile, young lady, you better get some rest, or I'll have to check you into the hospital!"

Raymond drove her to her apartment. On the way, she filled him in on the doctor's report.

In her home, she had barely undressed, preparing to collapse wearily into bed, when the phone rang. There was something angry in the sound of the bell.

She picked up the instrument. Her heart lurched at the now familiar deep, resonant voice of Jess Clark. He sounded coldly furious. "Lady, when I met you I thought you had the nature of a chilly iceberg. But I didn't figure you to be downright rude."

"Jess—"

"I'm not used to being stood up. Or maybe the little matter of our date to go sight-seeing this morning just happened to slip your mind?"

"Jess, if you'd let me explain—"

"What I can't figure out," he went on, too boiling mad to let her speak, "is why you'd pull a disappearing act like this when you're trying to sell me on the notion of representing your guitars. If this is the way your company does business, maybe we'd better forget the whole thing!"

A cold hand squeezed her heart. Surely he wouldn't be so petty as to pull out of the agreement over a personal misunderstanding! Or would he? His ego might be that delicately balanced. Considering the bleak struggles of his past, his must be an ego based on insecurity.

"I've had a heck of a time running you down," he went on, fuming. "First I came here to the hotel after canceling some important meetings just so I could have the day free to show you around the city. When I get here, the desk clerk informs me that you went charging out of here in the middle of the night. He said you told him something about going back to Tampa. I was sure you'd left a message of explanation for me. 'Not a thing,' he said, leaving me standing here like an idiot. I called Tampa, starting with the guitar factory, finally squeezed your apartment number out of them. . . ."

He seemed to run out of breath.

"Are you through?" she asked coldly.

"I suppose you have some kind of explanation for this crazy stunt?"

"Yes I have, and if you'll keep quiet for one minute, I'll give it to you." She drew a breath, making an effort to control her own anger. "First, I do apologize for not leaving a message for you. That was inconsiderate of me. But there just wasn't much time. And I was too upset to think clearly. I was planning to call you today to explain what happened. I got a call late last night from Tampa. My grandfather had a heart attack and was in intensive care. Naturally I rushed to the airport and grabbed the first available plane back to Tampa.''

There was a long silence. She heard a faint humming in the instrument held to her ear. When Jess spoke again, there was a remarkable change in the tone of his voice. ''Well, lady, I guess I'm the one who has some tall apologizing to do,'' he said with sincere humbleness. ''I really made a horse's north end out of myself, but I hope you can understand how things looked from my end.''

''Yes,'' she replied, her voice still chilly. ''However, I do think you could have waited for an explanation before you started chewing me out like that.''

''You're absolutely right, Andrea.''

''Are you always that hotheaded?''

''Not usually. Generally speaking it takes considerably more to get me in a fighting mood. Now I feel kind of foolish. I'm standing here trying to figure it out. It must be you.''

''I—I don't understand.''

''Well, in most cases if a woman stood me up, I'd just laugh it off and figure she wasn't worth raising my blood pressure over. Why did I get so steamed up this time? Was the difference you?''

There was another silence. The question disconcerted her. Was he expecting an answer? She couldn't give him one because she, too, was disturbed by how volatile their emotions were. It seemed as if their relationship were a volcano that was constantly boiling under the surface, ready to erupt at the slightest provocation.

He sounded genuinely concerned when he asked, "How is your grandfather?"

"I just came from the hospital. The doctor has reassured me that he's out of immediate danger. Apparently it was an attack brought on by business worries."

She couldn't resist that barb, hoping it might make him feel guilty enough to relent and sign the contracts.

But he appeared to ignore the arrow. "I'm glad to hear he's doing better. How long will you be in Tampa?"

"A few more days, then I'll fly back to Nashville."

"Good. Then we can take up where we left off."

A hot flush reddened her cheeks. There was a disturbing implication that he was referring to their personal involvement. She made an effort to get on safer ground. "Yes," she said in her best businesslike manner. "I'd like to resume negotiations on the contracts."

His chuckle was unnerving. "I wasn't exactly thinking about business matters. When you come back, maybe we can go on that sight-seeing trip around the city."

"Yes . . . all right."

Another tense silence. Then, "Well, let me know the minute you get back, Andrea. Meanwhile, I hope your grandfather will continue to improve."

"Thank you. . . ."

There was a soft click.

Andrea lay down to stare at the ceiling. She dozed fitfully, disturbed by dreams of a man in cowboy boots with a guitar slung over his shoulders, grabbing her up and riding off on a giant steed.

When she returned to the hospital that afternoon, she

was pleased to find that her grandfather had been moved from the IC unit to a private room. He wasn't immediately aware of her presence when she carefully cracked open the door of the sunny, cheerful room and peeked in silently in case he was asleep.

He lifted a hand and rested it over his eyes for a moment and she knew he was awake.

Her throat caught at his frailty. He had never been a big man. In younger years, his physique had been that of the slender aristocrat. Now the patrician thinness had wasted away, a weight loss it couldn't afford. His face was lined with sunken shadows under the high cheekbones. The effect seemed to have enlarged his ears and sharpened the aquiline thrust of his thin, straight nose. He had often reminded her, when he was younger, of a drawing she had seen of a Spanish conquistador, his mahogany-shaded visage fierce and hawklike under the plumed, half-melon helmet.

He moved his hand slowly from his face, the light catching the glaze of skin and blueness of vein. He had sensed her presence; his head turned in her direction.

She slipped into the room, pressing the door closed behind her.

"Abuelo!" She managed, after a hard swallow, to get a spark of brightness in the greeting. "How are you doing?"

His evenly contoured eyebrows lifted. His forehead was high, lifting to a widow's peak from which his thick sweep of silver hair lay in soft waves. She was relieved to see a vital spark in his eyes.

His eyes dwelled on her with an affection that brought a quiet little pain to her heart. "Andrea, sweetheart." He extended a hand, which she quickly held. Then awareness came to his eyes. A frown slashed his brow. "What in the devil are you doing here? You're supposed to be in Nashville."

"Raymond called last night to say that you'd gotten sick. I flew back."

"That Raymond," the old man growled fiercely. "I'll fire him immediately! How dare he call you in the middle of the night like that, making you fly all the way back here over nothing. I just had a little case of indigestion."

"You're not going to fire Raymond," she chided gently. "He loves you."

"He's a darn fool, getting everyone stirred up like this. I'll be out of here in the morning. Where's that idiot doctor, anyway? What did they do with my clothes? Look what they put on me!" He pulled the sheet down slightly, revealing a hospital gown. "This is something for a woman!"

Andrea suppressed a smile, relieved that the old man was feeling well enough to demonstrate some irascibility.

"Take it easy, Abuelo. I'll get some pajamas for you."

"Why?" demanded her grandfather. "I'm not going to be here long enough to put them on."

"I'm afraid you'll have to stay here a few days."

"Nonsense! They need me down at the factory. That new shipment of spruce came in."

He made an effort to sit up, but fell back against the pillow, looking baffled and frustrated. "I don't know why I feel so weak!" He said it as if in anger at himself.

"That's why you need to rest a few days, until you get your strength back."

"I don't have the time," he grumbled. Then he shot a

scowl around the room. "Where are my cigars? I can't find anything. They've put my clothes somewhere, hid my cigars. . . ."

Andrea shuddered at the thought of the storm that was going to erupt when the old gentleman was informed that he had smoked his last panatela.

They were interrupted by a nurse who entered on whispering crepe soles. She was carrying a tray that held a hypodermic needle.

"What's that for?" Manola Castille demanded, eyeing the instrument with dark suspicion.

"Just a little medication the doctor ordered," replied the nurse. She sponged a place on his arm with alcohol-saturated cotton. "This won't hurt," she promised and jabbed him before he could voice the protest rising to his lips.

The white-uniformed young woman gave Andrea a meaningful glance. "Only a few more minutes, Miss Castille. The doctor wants him to rest."

"Yes, I'll leave soon." Andrea nodded.

The nurse left. Manola grumbled, "Don't pay any attention to her. But you should get back to Nashville, sweetheart. I assume the contract is still without a signature?"

"Yes," she admitted reluctantly.

"Don't give up. Keep after them."

She forced a note of optimism into her voice. "I'm sure it's only a matter of another day or two, Abuelo. Just as soon as the business manager is back in town. . . ." But secretly, she cursed Jess Clark for his stubbornness about the contracts.

"I hope so. His signature will stave off the wolves, buy

us some time. I can show the contracts to my creditors, tell them of the big promotion we're planning. It will give us more financing, a fresh start for the company. Otherwise . . ."

"Abuelo, don't think about those things now," she urged softly. "Think about resting and getting well."

But he went doggedly on, muttering to himself as much as to her. "Otherwise, before the year is out we'll have to let them all go, the people who have been so loyal . . . the people. It's not just an old loft factory! They are not only employees. They are friends, my family. When they are gone and the door is locked, an era in the world of music will be gone forever."

She wasn't aware of moving, but she was suddenly pressing her young cheek to the parched old one, squeezing his hand. *"Mi abuelo,* we'll sell guitars door to door, strum them on street corners until people hear and appreciate the sound!"

"Of course, Andrea . . . we'll never let the sound die."

His mumbling grew indistinct as the sedative took effect. His voice faded to silence and he slept peacefully. Andrea gave his brow a tender kiss and tiptoed out of the room.

On her way back to her apartment, Andrea stopped at a shopping center to purchase some needed toiletries. She found a convenient parking place, locked her car and crossed to a sidewalk. On her way to the drugstore, she passed a record store.

Suddenly, Jess Clark's face leaped out at her.

She froze in her tracks, staring wide-eyed at the display in the store window. Several of Jess's albums were being featured. In every one were those lean, tanned features, those startling dark eyes gazing directly into hers.

During the tension-filled hours since Raymond's call last night, Jess and Nashville had seemed far away. She had been insulated from her emotions about him by worry over her grandfather.

Now, like a sudden blow to her stomach, everything Jess Clark had done to her emotional stability returned in a rush. Gazing at the record albums, she felt the same threatening impact she had felt the first time she had seen his publicity photographs. But now it was intensified by the personal contact she'd had with him.

She had not wanted to think about his lips, but the memory was back, burning her mouth. Her veins throbbed with the memory of the desire his embrace had awakened in her. How could she have forgotten? How could she ever forget?

As if Jess had followed her, she heard his voice, reinforcing her burning memory. She was so shocked her face whitened. Then she realized it was a phonograph in the store, playing one of his records. The voice tantalized her with an earthy, seductive song about a man and his woman, how she let her hair down and turned down the bedroom lights while the trucks went by outside and a honky-tonk across the street "played a lovin' song."

In a kind of trance, she moved into the record store. Feeling dazed, she pointed to the album on a rack behind the counter. The title was "Play Me a Lovin' Song." She opened her purse. The next thing she knew, she was back in her car, clutching the album, the real purpose of her stopping here forgotten.

She felt frightened by the intensity of her feelings.

Never had she felt so alive or so threatened. It was like a drug addict who had been high the night before and was having some kind of flashback. How was it possible? She had thought she'd left all that behind, something to be faced again when she returned to Nashville, but certainly nothing to haunt her here in the safety of Tampa.

Was there no escaping the man?

She hardly remembered driving to her apartment. She put the record album, still wrapped, on a table. *I'm not going to play it,* she thought. She was furious with herself for buying the thing. What had possessed her to buy an album of country-western songs? That kind of music was an anathema to her. She resented bitterly a fate that was forcing Castille Guitars to stoop to an alliance with this kind of music in order to survive. If it were up to her alone, she'd close the factory before associating the proud name of Castille with Jess Clark's Nashville music.

As if to protect herself, she put one of her favorite Segovia tapes on her stereo system, *Des Impresiones Levantinas.* She busied herself with a manicure as the exquisite talent of the master guitarist filled her apartment with cascading melody.

But she was distracted by the package on the table. She looked away. It drew back her gaze relentlessly.

Finally, with a muttered exclamation, she switched off the tape machine. Then she tore the wrapping from the album with angry rips.

"Forgive me, Segovia," she pleaded, and put the record on her turntable.

Now it was Jess's voice that filled the room. It was a record of love ballads. His was an artistry of another kind, one she did not understand or appreciate. But the impact of that rich voice and the seductive lyrics were inescapable.

She stretched out on her bed, listening. It was as if Jess were in the room singing directly to her alone. Was that the secret of his magic? Did every woman sense this intimacy in his voice and respond with quickened pulse?

"Play me a lovin' song. . . ."

Andrea stirred languorously on the bed. Her eyes were closed. Her loosened hair spilled around her flushed face. Her breathing was heavy. Her arms ached. She hugged a pillow. Her tongue touched her lips where they burned from the imprint of his kiss. The endless desire had awakened in her again, stronger than ever.

How could she fight this obsession?

A dreadful question assailed her.

Could she be falling in love with Jess Clark?

Her eyes flew open wide. "No!" she gasped aloud, shocked out of her reverie. It couldn't be! She'd analyzed her feelings rationally only last night in Nashville; it was just an infatuation.

Before she could search her mind and feelings any further, the telephone jarred her back to the mundane world.

She drew a shaky breath. A shudder went through her. She drew her hand across her forehead as if to brush away the confusion and reached for the instrument.

It was Raymond. "Hi. How did you find your grandfather?"

She swallowed and made a conscious effort to sound normal. "He was awake. I thought that, everything considered, he looked pretty good. He's mad because they won't give him his clothes and they hid his cigars."

Raymond chuckled. "That's a good sign."

"I thought so. We're going to have a devil of a time keeping him in the hospital, though."

"Let's hope the doctor can talk some sense into him. He has a lot of respect for Racklin."

There was a short pause, then Raymond said, "Aside from wanting to hear about your grandfather, I had another reason for calling. Could you have dinner with me this evening, Andrea? I have something important I want to talk with you about."

She frowned, forgetting for the moment her turmoil over Jess Clark. "Of course, Raymond. But what is it?"

"I—I really can't discuss it over the phone."

There was a note of tension in his voice.

"All right, then. Dinner will be fine. What time?"

"Suppose I pick you up about seven."

"I'll be ready."

She hung up, feeling puzzled.

Chapter Eight

$\mathcal{A}$ndrea shook off the spell she had fallen under while listening to Jess's record. She went about the business of getting ready for her dinner date with Raymond, determined to put Nashville and Jess out of her mind for the evening.

From her closet, she chose a simple black dress and arranged her long hair in French braids that framed the pale oval of her face and imparted a stylish effect.

As she dressed, she puzzled over Raymond's phone call.

There had been an element of mystery in his message. What was so important that he couldn't discuss it over the phone? It wouldn't be a matter concerning her grandfather's illness; he would have relayed that to her immediately. Could it have to do with the Nashville situation?

Had Jess Clark or his business manager contacted Raymond?

Perhaps that was it!

By the time Raymond knocked on her door, she had about convinced herself that was the reason for their dinner date.

She managed to make perfunctory replies to his polite conversation as they drove through the streets of Tampa, but her mind had strayed many miles away, to the city of Nashville. What was Jess doing now, playing before a concert audience, singing in a recording studio, having another cookout at the Quackendalls? Or was he somewhere alone with Nori, holding her in his arms, kissing her as he had kissed Andrea only last night? The thought brought hot waves of anger surging through her. *Good Lord, I'm jealous,* she thought hopelessly. What an emotional trap she had fallen into! On the one hand, she hated Jess Clark for a number of reasons, among them the delay he was causing over the contracts and the ruthless conquest he was making of her emotions. On the other hand, she missed him terribly, felt despair over his involvement with Nori and yearned constantly for the touch of his hand, his embrace that set her ablaze with desire.

"You're very pensive tonight," Raymond said.

His voice startled her out of her introspective thoughts. "Sorry, I didn't mean to be antisocial. Just thinking about some things."

With an effort, she gained control of her turbulent emotions. "Why were you so mysterious over the phone, Raymond? What did you want to tell me?"

He smiled. "I'll tell you over dinner."

"Does it have something to do with the Jess Clark contracts? Did his business manager call you?"

Raymond looked surprised. "No, did you expect they would?"

"Not exactly. I was trying to figure out what it was that was so important. I just thought maybe—"

"Well, one of the reasons I wanted to see you tonight was to hear about your progress with Jess Clark, though that isn't the main reason."

Andrea sighed. "I'm afraid *progress* isn't exactly the best word to describe how things are going, Raymond. We've run into a stone wall—which is the best way to describe Jess Clark's stubbornness!" A mingling of anger and despair brought a rush of stinging tears.

Raymond's gaze left the road for a moment to give her a worried glance. "But I thought everything was settled! The last conversation I had with his business manager was cordial and agreeable. He was satisfied with the terms spelled out in the contracts. We were all under the impression that your going to Nashville was just a formality for the signing of the agreements."

"That's what I thought," she said bitterly. "Unfortunately, the high and mighty Jess Clark decided to review the business deal you and his business manager worked out. Suddenly he's thrown a monkey wrench in the machinery."

"I don't understand."

"Raymond, he isn't satisfied with just a payoff for his services in promoting Castille guitars. He wants a partnership in the company!"

For a moment, Raymond appeared too surprised to reply. Then in a dazed voice, he asked, "A partnership?"

"Exactly. He doesn't want any money at all. He says he wants to own a part of Castille Guitars. He claims that as a partner he can do more for the company in the way of promotion and financing and that he'd be more dedicated to the project. I can't make up my mind if he's sincere about that, or if he just wants the prestige of being closely involved with an aristocratic name like Castille, or if it's plain old greed."

Raymond slowly shook his head. "Your grandfather would never agree to those kinds of terms."

"I know," she said hopelessly.

"Does he want a full partnership?"

"He says he won't insist on an equal partnership. He seems to be open to negotiations on how much ownership he'd have."

"Hmm." Raymond frowned thoughtfully. "There could be some advantages in that for us. As a partner, the Jess Clark organization would certainly open a lot of doors for us, to say nothing of the unlimited financing. . . ."

"But Raymond, you know Grandfather would never agree! Forget about the practical side. Our family name is involved. The proud name of Castille has stood behind the quality of our instruments for generations. To make it public that a country-western singer has taken over part of the company would be the final straw that would kill Grandfather."

Raymond nodded soberly. "You're right, of course. I was just thinking aloud. Considering your grandfather's present state of health, the heart attack and all, I wouldn't even want to mention it to him. On the other hand, if Jess

Clark backs out of this deal, it's going to have serious consequences on your grandfather's health, too."

Andrea nodded, feeling the crushing weight of despair. "The way it stands now, it's a no-win situation. And it's Jess's fault! Somehow I have to convince him to drop this insane notion of a partnership and sign the original agreement."

"Do you think you can do that?"

"I certainly plan to try," she said grimly. "If he has an ounce of compassion, maybe I can get through to him."

Raymond took her to one of the fine old Spanish restaurants in the Ybor City section. They dined by candlelight in a courtyard, right next to a splashing fountain. An old-world Spanish atmosphere lingered in the balconies, the patios, the wrought-iron grillwork, the semitropical plants in this section of the city. It was reminiscent of the Vieux Carre in New Orleans.

The waiters were second generation in their profession, steeped in a tradition of excellence. The reasonable prices and high quality of the food and service had made the restaurant a Tampa tradition. Raymond gave their order, a dinner of black bean soup, Spanish mixed salad and paella valenciana.

Afterward they ordered demitasse—rich, black Cuban-style coffee.

"Raymond, I really can't bear this suspense any longer. You invited me out for dinner because you had something special to tell me. If it doesn't have anything to do with the Jess Clark negotiations, what is it? I've sensed all through dinner that you've been uptight."

He chuckled. "Is it that obvious?"

"Well, not obvious to other people, I don't think. But I know you so well, I'm aware of your moods."

He nodded slowly. "We do know each other pretty well, don't we?"

"Sure. You're like one of the family, Raymond. You know that." She thought back to when he had first joined the firm. "Let's see. It was five years ago when you started working for Grandfather, wasn't it?"

"That's right."

"I remember, I was still in college. I was very impressed by you. I thought you were so businesslike. You stepped right in and took some of the load off Grandfather at the factory. The details were getting beyond him. And some of the new things, the computers. Poor Abuelo. He'd never understand how to use them!"

Raymond smiled. "You'll never know how I had to argue with him to buy them."

There was a moment of silence.

"Remember the first time we had dinner here, Andrea?"

She nodded, her expressive eyes showing a fond glow for a time when life hadn't yet revealed itself as a vise with inexorable jaws.

"We had a lot to talk about that evening," he reminisced. "It was a fun time."

"Yes, Raymond, it was."

Raymond looked down at his coffee thoughtfully. Andrea knew he was carefully planning his next words. That was one of the things that was both solidly reassuring and irritatingly frustrating about Raymond Ayers. He would not be rushed into blurting out impetuous statements. He weighed his words, choosing them with great deliberation, making certain they conveyed exactly what he intended. She knew from experience there was no hurrying him at times like this. She sipped her coffee and tried to be patient.

He seemed to arrive at some agreement with his thoughts and looked up. "Andrea," he began, "I'm sure you know that I admire and respect you tremendously."

She stared at him, her puzzlement growing. "Yes, and I'm very fond of you, Raymond."

"I'm glad to hear that. I'm not sure if I've chosen the right time to talk to you about this. I mean, with your grandfather in the hospital, the business of Nashville unsettled. But I know you'll be going back to deal with the matter of the contracts as soon as you're sure your grandfather is out of danger and I wanted to tell you how I feel before you leave."

He fumbled in a pocket, then placed a small box on the table before her. He opened it and Andrea saw the sparkle of a large diamond.

"This is what I wanted to talk to you about, Andrea. I've been in love with you for a long, long time, maybe from the first time I met you. You were so young then, still in college, and I was trying to build a financial future. Over the years we've grown closer. I want you to be my wife, Andrea. I want you to marry me."

Andrea wasn't sure if she gasped aloud. Raymond's proposal didn't come as a complete surprise. She had suspected, with a woman's intuition about such things, that Raymond had been getting serious about her for some time. Nevertheless she felt temporarily stunned. A proposal is a momentous occasion in a woman's life. She wasn't prepared for it tonight.

As her friendship with Raymond had grown over the years, she had neither encouraged nor discouraged him, not being sure of her own heart. It was true that she was very fond of Raymond. There were many things about him that she found reassuring and attractive. They had dated fairly regularly, though there had been no talk about an understanding or going steady. They shared many common interests—classical music, the theater, world politics. Andrea was more sports-minded, liking tennis, horseback riding, water sports. Other than an occasional golf game, Raymond was wrapped up in business. But he had a good mind. She enjoyed the lengthy discussions they got into, ranging from philosophy to current events.

There was no reason why she shouldn't marry him. A week ago, she probably would have said yes. It would be a good marriage. They agreed on the important things, a home life, children. Raymond would be a dependable, solid source of strength through the years.

But between last week and tonight, there had been Nashville and a kiss that had wracked her world, had ignited fires she never knew existed, had promised delights and a fulfillment beyond her wildest fantasies. But with the promises, there lurked the ever-present threat of a crushing heartbreak more devastating than she had believed possible.

Raymond, why didn't you ask me last week? Why did you let me go to Nashville? Life with you would be so much simpler! It would be sane! It would be safe!

Yes, but would it turn out to be the plains now that she had glimpsed the mountaintops?

The coward in her wanted to say yes even now. Going

back to Nashville wearing Raymond's engagement ring would protect her from Jess Clark. Or would it? Would anything protect that fatal weakness in her that responded so avidly to Jess's magnetic attraction? How could she wear Raymond's engagement ring, knowing full well that if Jess got her in a compromising situation again, she'd weaken?

She struggled with her breath. Her stricken gaze rushed to Raymond's face. "Raymond, I hardly know what to say. I didn't expect this."

He looked surprised. "You didn't? Surely you must have realized for some time that I've been falling in love with you."

"Yes. What I mean is, I didn't expect a proposal tonight. I—I'm not sure of my own thoughts. So much has been happening. The problems with the business, the Nashville thing, Grandfather's heart attack."

She reached across the table for Raymond's hand. Her eyes pleaded with him to understand. "Can we talk about this another time?"

He nodded slowly, disappointment clearly registered in his eyes. He sighed. "I really didn't pick a good time, as I said. I thought I should have waited. But I didn't want you going back to Nashville without knowing how I felt. You know, Andrea, we could have a good marriage. I can take care of you. I'm going to do everything in my power to save your grandfather's business. But if everything fails and the factory closes, I'll be able to provide you with security. I've made some good real estate investments along with other things. We'd have a lot going for us."

"I know, Raymond. I have every confidence in you.

It's not that. It's just that when I get married, I want to be absolutely sure of my own feelings. Right now I'm not sure of anything.''

She paused, biting her lip. Then she said, ''All I know for sure right now is that as soon as Grandfather is out of danger, I must go back to Nashville. . . .''

Chapter Nine

Her hotel room had an added air of uncertainty as she entered it. Three days had elapsed since she had left so suddenly to fly to Tampa. Now she was back. What changes had occurred in her absence? Had Jess Clark's business manager returned? Or was nothing changed?

She gazed at the telephone as soon as she closed the door. It lurked on the bedside table hypnotically, like a potential enemy on a leash.

She would shower and freshen up, giving herself a little time to calm down after the flight. Then she knew she would have to call Jess. That was unavoidable. The implications involved unnerved her.

The desk clerk had welcomed her back with a smile when she'd climbed from the airport taxi and crossed the delightful cavern of the hotel lobby.

He'd consulted the pigeonhole that had the number of her room. No, there had been no messages.

Now she hurried through the act of showering and changing into a summery soft yellow A-line skirt and blouse. In her attaché case was the list of several telephone numbers where Castille Guitars had reached Jess Clark during the contract negotiations.

She examined the list. It included his business manager, his attorney, the executive secretary in a music publishing company where Jess owned a block of stock sufficient to warrant his personal attention in the daily decisions and running of the company. There were also unlisted private home numbers he'd deigned to give out.

Gathering her courage, she tried the first number. The business manager's secretary informed her that Mr. Clark was not there. Further questioning revealed the crushing news that the business manager was still out of town.

The secretary, noting the disappointment in Andrea's voice, suggested, "You might try CQ Records, Miss Castille. I think Mr. Clark called a staff meeting over there to discuss some recording-session scheduling."

"Thank you."

At CQ her call was relayed from a switchboard to an executive assistant's office where a secretary said that Mr. Clark was in the building but tied up in a meeting. "Give me your number and I'll have him return your call, Miss Castille."

Andrea gave the number and hung up pensively, thinking of the way the secretary, a stranger, had addressed her, something in her tone implying that Andrea wasn't a stranger at all. Andrea wondered how much the Music Row grapevine knew about her. There were not many secrets on the Row, she was sure. Was she, already, emerging as Jess Clark's latest tumble? Word of such sultry beauty would have gotten around as soon as Peewee Sloan had dropped into one of his favorite haunts after meeting her at the airport. Anything relevant to Jess was an instant morsel flashing from mouth to mouth, chuckle to wink. What had Jess himself said among his cronies? Were the gossips making book on how long it would take Jess to make this new conquest?

Her cheeks flamed at the humiliating suspicions. Was she being too paranoid? But then, maybe she wasn't! Why had fate sentenced her to an involvement with a man of Jess's reputation with women? It robbed her of privacy, thrust her into the gossip column limelight. How much more dignified and respectable for her to have accepted Raymond's proposal and settled down to a quiet, normal life and predictable routine.

The minutes crawled while she awaited the return of her call. She caught herself pacing the plush carpet. She tried to concentrate on the view from her window, the stately and historic buildings housing the functions of state government, the impressive functionalism of art and entertainment, the curve of the Cumberland curling like a protective motherly arm around its child, Nashville, the green of cool woods, meadows and farmland carpeting a gently rolling countryside that stretched to a distant horizon.

She settled in a comfortable club chair and opened a book, reading the words while her true attention focused on the telephone. Once, she looked at her watch, certain the hands were no longer moving, and lifted it to her ear to see if it was still ticking.

She felt sure the secretary had given Jess Clark the number. Anxiety piled on top of frustration. Damn! Had her sudden departure robbed her of her place in the line of petitioners struggling to see him? Perhaps she had been swallowed in the hue and cry rattling for his attention. Maybe the delays and put-offs and you'll-have-to-call-back-later that had strung out the negotiations and driven her grandfather up the wall hadn't been deliberate slights after all. Maybe so many constant demands were made on Jess Clark's time that he hadn't been able to help the endless delays.

Now she had become a victim of that time pressure.

Finally she stretched on her back on the bed, simply waiting and wishing the silence wasn't so endless.

A new fear assailed her. What if an invisible door were slowly creaking closed? What if he decided the Castille Guitars matter was, after all, just not worth his valuable time and effort?

What if—

The ringing of the phone was a sudden explosion. She bounded up, catching a glimpse of her face in the mirror, strained and pale. She was conscious of the quick fluttering of her heart, the catch of breath in her throat.

Ninny! she chided herself. She stood for a moment, drawing a deep breath, making a conscious effort to calm down.

Then she was at the phone, quietly lifting it on the third buzz.

"Hello?"

"Andrea."

It was a statement, not a question. The sound of his voice sent a surge of adrenaline through her veins.

"Yes, hello, Jess," she said in a voice more even than she had believed she could possibly manage. "Thank you for returning my call. I've come back from Tampa and I want to see if we can resume negotiations on the contract."

He chuckled softly in a way that irritated her. Was there an element of mockery in his amused response? What did he mean by it?

He ignored her mention of the contract. Instead, turning serious, he asked, "How is your grandfather?"

"Much better. The doctor assured me he was out of danger, so I felt it all right to return."

"That's good."

What? That her grandfather was better, or that she had returned? She couldn't ask. Instead, she said, "I phoned your business manager's office when I was trying to reach you this morning. His secretary said he still hasn't gotten back into town."

"I know. I'm sorry."

"Jess, there have been so many delays!"

"It won't be much longer now," he promised. "I talked to him last night. I feel sure he'll be able to leave there by the end of the week."

Several more days! Her reaction was mixed, disappointment over the contracts, but at the same time a sudden throb of her pulse at the prospect of a reason to spend a few more days in this city with Jess.

She gathered her resolve and made a fresh approach to the matter of the contracts. "Jess, are you still going to insist on a partnership as a condition to signing the agreement?"

"Well, Andrea, it seems the best for all of us. As a

partner, I could offer your company a lot more. Y'know, Jess Clark Enterprises has its fingers in a lot of pies, all of which would benefit Castille Guitars. And I'd feel a whole lot more dedicated to saving the company.''

''I know, you've already explained all that to me. But can't you try to see our side of this? I realize it's difficult to explain my grandfather's kind of old-world family pride. Making guitars is more than a business with him. It's—well, it's all involved with family and self-respect and holding his head up in his community. His father, his grandfather, his great-grandfather all put the stamp of their exclusive name on our instruments. . . .''

Her voice failed. Words were so inadequate to explain her grandfather's viewpoint! Manola Castille and Jess Clark were totally alien to each other, men from different generations, different worlds.

''I don't mean to sound harsh,'' Jess replied, ''but all that family pride stuff isn't going to do him a whole lot of good if the business goes bust. Did you talk to him about my proposition?''

''Heavens, no! Not in his precarious state of health. I just told him there were some delays until your business manager came back. I did discuss it with Raymond Ayers, the plant manager. He agreed that there would be some very direct benefits to us, as you pointed out. But he also agreed that Grandfather would never accept that kind of arrangement and to bring it up now could impede his recovery.''

There was a moment of silence as Jess apparently considered her words. Finally he said, ''Andrea, why don't we drop all this for now. Obviously we're not going to solve anything. Wait until my business manager gets back and we'll tackle the problem then. Meanwhile I'll have that chance to show you some more of Nashville. We can have a late lunch after we prowl around town to work up an appetite.''

Andrea felt the crushing weight of disappointment and frustration. Trying to change Jess Clark's mind was like trying to move a three-ton boulder. She had never met such a stubborn man!

She was thankful it was a telephone conversation so he couldn't see the tears of grief and anger trickling down her cheeks. She was hearing the death knell of Castille Guitars. Jess wouldn't budge from his demands for a partnership. Her grandfather would never agree. It was the end of the company. Her mission had failed.

''You're so busy,'' she said coldly. ''I'm sure you can't find time. . . .''

She was sure he heard the anger in her voice, but he chose to ignore it. ''Heck,'' he said, ''I'm always snowed, Andrea. If I want time, I have to make it. Important things come first. I can take a few hours for myself without going bankrupt. You only live once and I made up my mind a long time ago that I wasn't going to turn myself into a slave over this money-making thing the way so many guys do.''

He suddenly laughed as if he'd remembered something very amusing. ''You ever hear of an old novelty song called 'I Don't Want to Be the Richest Man in the Cemetery'?''

''No,'' she said, her tone still icy. How would she possibly know something like that?

''Well, anyway,'' he said, still chuckling, ''the singer is saying that he can't see the point of spending all his time getting rich if hard work is going to put him in an early grave. Y'know, some of those songs have real good, practical advice. A lot of my friends have done just that, spent all their time chasing around in circles to make money, then keeled over before they turned forty. To heck with that. I like money as much as the next guy, and the good Lord has been real generous to me on that score. But I plan to stop now and then to enjoy life along the way.''

He was showing her a new side of Jess Clark again, a kind of happy-go-lucky, totally relaxed man, able to shed the demands put on the pop music superstar and return to being a carefree kid again. Perhaps it was a throwback to his hobo days, maybe even a nostalgic longing for those less complicated times.

His lighthearted manner was having a melting effect on her, like a spring sun thawing frost. It was difficult to remain angry with him when he turned on that irresistible Jess Clark charm full force. Her feeling of despair began to dissipate. A measure of hope returned. Perhaps all was not yet lost. Nothing was to be gained by throwing up her hands in surrender. She could be as stubborn as he!

A fresh wave of resolve swept through her. She wasn't going to give up! She'd stay here until he changed his mind. Meanwhile, she determined to put family and business worries aside until his business manager returned. Until then, she would get to know Jess Clark better. She would enjoy his company. Perhaps the way to melting his stubborn heart was through their growing friendship.

She stirred in the chair, feeling a heady movement in her blood, a feathery pulse in her throat, an awareness of the loveliness of the summer day, a languorous suspension of time.

"Well," she said, relenting, "if you think you have the time, I would like to see some more of your city. . . ."

"Great! That makes two of us itching to break out of the starting gate. How soon can you be ready?"

"Actually, I'm dressed now. Casual. Nothing fancy."

"Makes it perfect."

"Where are you?"

"Where do you think? Downstairs. I'm calling from the lobby."

"I see. You seem to have been pretty sure of my reaction."

"Why not? You have to believe in things you want."

"Oh, you do? Do I detect a note of arrogance in that statement?"

"Arrogance? Heck, no. But you always have to be careful about what you're wishing for, because you're liable to get it. If you're going to make your dreams come true, you have to be like a kid—believe in Santa Claus, in tomorrow, in yourself and your ability to turn your dream into reality. The world is full of long-faced failures who forgot how to do that."

Now he was being the philosopher. Was it simply a cover-up for arrogance? she wondered. She supposed he had to have a certain amount of that to rise out of the slag heaps, to find his star and reach for it. Jess Clark: gentle philosopher, brawler, poet, fraud, gutter tough, self-educated, earthy and worldly. He was all of those things and more. What else more? What were the things she didn't know about him? The question held a fascination.

But she wasn't going to get the answers by hanging on the telephone. "Are we going to sit here and discuss philosophy over the phone or are we going sight-seeing?"

She could almost see his grin. "That's my girl. Grab the nearest elevator. I'm waiting."

He was right in front of the elevator when the doors opened, smiling and reaching for her hand before she'd stepped all the way out.

She'd almost forgotten her nervousness about how it would be when she saw him again. But she hadn't been entirely able to prepare herself for the impact of seeing him before her, of touching his hand. Electricity flowed. Arteries pumped. Skin flushed. Once again, she felt that intoxicating sensation of being more alive than ever before in her life. It was overwhelming!

"Welcome back, you lovely woman. The glow has returned to Nashville."

And to me, she thought secretly. In spite of the anger she had felt only a few minutes before, he could still do this to her. She had wondered all the way back to Nashville if she would feel the same magic when they met again. She had the answer in the rapid tempo of her heartbeat, the tingling that raced through her body.

She laughed nervously. "Flattery will get you anywhere—almost."

"Who's flattering?"

He was holding both her hands, making her both self-conscious and pleased by a long, appraising survey, his black-eyed gaze raking her from head to foot with a kind of visual embrace. Coals smoldered in his eyes as he drank in the sight of her with total concentration, as if the entire universe were pinpointed in her being. He appeared completely oblivious to anything or anyone else around them. If they were the object of curious stares, he was unconscious of them.

Was he thinking of that night in the swimming pool, their almost nude bodies locked in passionate embrace, the eager, hungry, demanding kiss? The expression in his eyes told her he was. Hot blood rushed to her face. Nervously, she drew her hands from his.

Today, to hide his identity from the crowds on the sidewalk who might mob them, he had replaced his usual western-style clothes for a sport shirt, slacks and sandals. The outfit seemed ridiculously incongruous on him. She had wondered with bit of secret amusement if he slept with his boots on. To complete the deception, Jess donned large, mirrorlike reflective sunglasses and pulled a hat down low over his forehead.

"What do you think?"

"If I didn't know better, I'd take an oath you were a tourist."

"Hope you're right," he said grimly. "If somebody spots me, we could get stampeded."

He took her arm and started in the direction of the outer doors. When they were on the sidewalk, he paused.

"Where would you like to start?" he asked. "You have quite a range of choices. Nashville isn't altogether country music. This town is also called the Protestant Vatican of the South. More churches per capita than any other American City. It has the biggest payroll in religious publishing from prayer cards and hymnals to monthly magazines. And then there are the massive banking and insurance companies. Some call it the Wall Street of the South.''

''Well, all that sounds interesting but slightly dull for such a gorgeous, sunny day. How about the Jess Clark part of Nashville?''

''Music Row? Fine with me. But we can't do it in a single morning. That's a lot crowded into a few square blocks. Columbia Studio is the site that began Music Row when Owen Bradley opened a recording studio in 1955. There's the Country Music Hall of Fame and Museum, where you can see the instruments and costumes of the great. In the Nashville songwriters' hall of fame there are portraits of members, original manuscripts, a potpourri of memorabilia. Then there's Elvis-A-Rama in light and sound. There's the Country Music Wax Museum.

''For starters you might like to see the Upper Room Chapel, an adaptation of the room depicted in Leonardo da Vinci's 'The Last Supper.' ''

''How many are you in?''

''What? Jails? Fleabags?''

''You know what I mean! Those halls of fame. Would I see your manuscripts in the songwriters' museum? Maybe a guitar you've played in the Country Music Hall of Fame? Or would I run face-on into you in lifelike wax sculpture?''

''You might,'' he admitted with a lean grin. ''You might even decide I look better in wax.''

Not much chance of that! she thought, giving his lean, broad-shouldered physique a sidewise glance and feeling her heart lurch.

''Could we just wander a little?'' she suggested. ''Not

have a starting or stopping point, just kind of be like gawking tourists, sort of soak up the scene where you operate?''

"Sure. You'll see several nice, modern, functional buildings—''

"But I'll see people," she said. "Their faces, the way they hurry or dawdle, and I can make up stories about them. I'll let my imagination roam.''

He gave her a warm-eyed look. "Did anybody ever tell you you're marvelous?''

No, but you may, she thought. Being with him, she was alive again. She wasn't going to spoil this morning with a lot of heavy agonizing about her feelings. It was good to be with him, better than anything else she could imagine. She would leave it at that for now. Worry about the consequences later when it was too late and he'd left her with a heartache greater than she could bear. A sudden chill made her shiver. But she resolutely put those dark thoughts aside for another time.

They drifted along streets she would remember: South, Music Square East, Hawkins, Music Square West. The magic of millions upon millions of dollars had wiped clean the disease of inner-city decay and erected commercial shrines and attractions in its stead. Busy, busy, busy was the tone. Smartly dressed young executives rubbed elbows with outlandish, sequined drugstore cowboys. There were those in runover boots and patched jeans, long hair and Mohawk haircuts. A girl rushed by clutching a bundle of dog-eared manuscripts. On a street corner stood a youth with a guitar on his back, looking around as if he weren't sure which way to go next. Someone was playing the "Wabash Cannon Ball" on a harmonica, one of the few content to dawdle along and let the torrent of humanity flow about him. There were faces young and old. There were eyes filled with the stuff of stars and eyes that were burned out like dead embers. Gawking tourists were being herded like sheep by a guide reciting a spiel he had uttered a thousand times.

A black limousine came to a stop at Decca Records. A blond girl dressed in fringed buckskin got out amidst a rush of people, and she waved and threw kisses as two burly bodyguards guided her through the crowd. There was a nasty catcall or two from frustrated autograph hounds and a souvenir snatched from the buckskin fringe as the girl was safely escorted past the security guards on her way to the recording session.

Andrea was thankful that so far Jess had been able to remain incognito with his sport clothes, eyeshades and a hat pulled low, protecting them from that kind of mob scene. She was nervous the whole time that someone was going to recognize him and start a stampede.

She had never before given much thought to what it would be like to be a celebrity. Now she was getting a taste of it, secondhand. One paid a high price for fame, never having a private life of one's own, not even being able to go for a simple sight-seeing or shopping trip without being mobbed. In a sense, Jess was a prisoner of his own success.

"Do you ever resent it?" she asked curiously. "Constantly being hounded by fans? Having to sneak around like you're doing now, hiding behind sunglasses?"

"It goes with the territory, I guess." He shrugged.

She gave him a quick, curious glance. Again she had run into a stone wall. He could be very talkative on almost any subject except what really went on inside Jess Clark. He was very voluble. He could talk endlessly about his music, his friends, the city. He could tell marvelous, amusing stories about his early experiences when he rode the rails and dodged flying bottles in honky-tonks. But when it came to talking about his own deeper feelings he was suddenly without words. That part remained silent, hidden. If pushed for an answer, he either brushed off the question with a flip remark or changed the subject.

She was beginning to think she would never know the real Jess Clark. There was an impenetrable barrier around the inner core of feelings. Either he was a very private person, or he simply did not know how to communicate those intensely personal experiences and feelings.

He might deliver a bit of drawling, homespun philosophy—"My ol' pappy always said that . . ."—with unspoken acknowledgment that he was playing with satire. But never did he speak of the agony of a young child seeing his daddy come out of the mines, eyes robbed of hope, coughing his life away. He'd make "we were so poor" jokes, laughing the whole time. "We were so poor the mice brought us cheese." But he never spoke of Christmas in a barren shack with no presents for a skinny, wistful-eyed urchin shivering from the wind blowing through the cracks.

From what she had read, it must have been that way for him. Had he forgotten? Had he through some sanity-protecting defense managed to blank it out? Or could he simply not talk about it? Boys with that background were taught to be stoic from childhood.

He interrupted her introspective thoughts. "You know something? I'm starved."

She laughed. "Thanks for reminding me. I've been so busy taking in the sights, I hadn't noticed I was famished."

"Glad we agree. Now I can suggest several good restaurants not far from here. . . ."

"I know where I'd like to go," she said impulsively. "That first day, when Peewee brought me from the airport, he talked about those places where you got your start when you first came here."

"You mean one of the cornbread and beans joints?"

"Yes. The very first place where you got a meal when you hit Nashville."

He chuckled, shaking his head. "Your stomach may hate you for that crazy impulse."

"Humor me. I feel adventurous today."

"Remember you asked for it. Old gal named Mom Laudermilk runs the place now. You're sure?"

"Absolutely."

"Okay." he shrugged resignedly. "Mom Laudermilk's, here we come!"

Geographically, the joint was but a short drive away in his Mercedes. But the evidence of entry into another world was apparent as the car turned into a depressed old street. Once fine houses had decayed into gloomy, forbidding hulks. There was a garage that looked more like a junkyard, a neighborhood grocery with steel bars over the dirty windows, a small turn-of-the-century park now a grassless, refuse-littered gathering place for shuffling winos and street people.

"Worse than a coal mine," he muttered. "Makes you wish you could do something to help."

She glanced at him. "Well, why don't you? You could afford to."

He said nothing, slowing the car as an old bewhiskered drunk staggered out of a gloomy bar and set an uncertain course for the other side of the street.

Watching his profile, she prodded, "From the things I've read and heard, Jess Clark is a soft touch. Charitable concerts, donations. I doubt if you keep everything for yourself."

He shrugged. "How could I? When there's such a flood I never could possibly spend it by myself. The good Lord wouldn't forgive me for that."

There it was again, that simple, humble gospel side of the country singer, sounding sincere enough for her to believe him. She continued looking at him, wondering at the puzzling complexities of the man. "Who gets your donations?" she pried. "Charities here or back home?"

He shrugged. Again that wall came down. There was nothing more. Just silence.

She sank into the luxury of the bucket seat, stealing a fresh study of the hawkish profile.

She'd already formed a mental inventory of Jess Clark: fraud, panther, tooth-and-claw survivor, homespun humorist, poet, a fiercely loyal friend, deadly enemy, humble gospel singer, colossal ego, earthy, woman charmer, gallant, polite, soft-spoken, two-fisted. She could add philanthropist to the list.

She glanced away. Human nature—territory where heaven and hell splashed and sometimes raged over each other. Who could understand it? More to the point, who could understand a man like Jess Clark?

"Last chance to trade mulligan stew for Alaskan king crab," he warned.

She looked about. They were in a blue-collar area, secondhand and thrift stores, cut-rate furniture and E-Z Credit used cars, weathered tenements, clapboard houses, storefront fundamental revival missions. Jess was wheeling the car into a dusty parking lot beside a barnlike building on the corner. He let the car drift slowly as he scanned for a space among the battered heaps, motorcycles and rusty pickup trucks and vans. He parked between a rust-eaten sedan with ancient tail fins and a bumperless Beetle.

Andrea's survey was one of quick interest as they crossed the lot to the sidewalk. The building that hulked on the corner was their destination. She could hear the insistent pound of rhythm from a jukebox as they neared the door. Across the front window, dirty with age, a sign spelled out EATS BY MOM LAUDERMILK. WELCOME. AIN'T NO STRANGERS.

Jess opened the door and they stepped through. The dimensions of the interior were as barnlike as the exterior had suggested. The place was crowded and noisy. Beer drinkers were strung along the bar to the right. The cash register was ringing steadily. Waitresses with laden trays moved with brisk efficiency, unaffected by the loud talk, the laughter, the confusion. The furnishings were farmhouse plain, designed for service and obviously aged to the point where they'd seen plenty. A pleasant, country-kitchen aroma mingled with the acrid smell of spilled, stale beer.

They no sooner entered than a large, stout woman

grabbed them both. "Lordy, it's good to see you, Jess," a husky contralto rasped in Andrea's ear, "but lemme get you where you won't be noticed or there'll be a commotion started and you won't be able to eat a bite." Quickly, she hustled them to a secluded booth in the rear.

Safely hidden from the other patrons, Jess removed his oversized sunglasses. "Didn't fool you, huh, Mom?"

"Not for a minute. Spotted you the second you walked in the door."

"I thought I was doing pretty good. We've been walking all over Nashville this morning. Not one person stopped me for an autograph. Mom, I want you to meet Andrea Castille."

The woman smiled warmly. She had big, square, porcelainlike teeth—obviously dentures. They clacked slightly when she talked. Her iron-gray hair was drawn tightly and worn in a bun on top of her head.

"Hello, dear. I'm Mom Laudermilk. I run this place." She extended a hand that might have belonged to a longshoreman except it was as soft as a big pillow and as smooth as if it had been steamed.

Andrea had taken a seat in the booth, but Jess, in deference to Mom Laudermilk, was still on his feet. Again that old-fashioned gallantry, Andrea thought. She wondered what a young, militant, urban women's libber would make of Jess. He was the type who would open a door for a woman if he had to knock her down to do it.

"Andrea, Mom is everybody's Mom. She stuffed me with a lot of hamburgers when I couldn't pay for them."

"Jess, shut up! You paid me back several times over since then," Mom growled.

"Why don't you take the load off your feet, Mom?"

"Yes," Andrea said, liking the big woman immensely. "If you can spare some rush-hour time, please join us."

"Aw, the place is geared to pretty well run itself. I'm just around to add the personal touch and see that the cashier doesn't steal me blind." She eased her iron-pumper's solidity into a straight-backed chair pulled up to the booth's table. Only then did Jess slide into a seat beside Andrea.

"You're a beautiful young woman," Mom Laudermilk said. "You got the coloring of a fine lady from Barcelona. I can just see you with a comb and one of them black lace mantillas in your hair."

"Truth is," Jess said, "Andrea does have the blood of royal Spanish ancestors flowing in her veins."

"That a fact, now?"

"Yes. Her family builds Castille guitars."

The large woman's expressive face registered awe. "Castille . . . Castille. I thought I'd heard that name before. Why, them's the finest instruments in the world!"

Andrea smiled, pleased that the reputation of the guitars would be respected even in a place like this. "I've flown to Nashville to get Jess's endorsement. We're planning a national promotion with him helping us increase our sales."

"Well, honey, you couldn't get a better endorsement. A man in Jess Clark's position can't shave in the morning without the whole town knowing if he nicked that heart-melting profile." Then she asked, "Where do you hail from, Andrea?"

"Tampa, Florida."

"Tampa. Now that's some town! Once I was there

during the week-long blowout they call Gasparilla. That was some festival. I don't reckon I slept a total of twelve hours that whole week. What part of Tampa do you live in?''

"I have an apartment in the Ybor City section."

"Ybor City. That's the Latin quarter, right?"

"Sounds like you know Tampa pretty well."

"My late husband and I used to book gigs on the Gulf coast. He played fiddle, I played a little steel guitar. We had a pretty solid little group. But you talk about Ybor City. I loved to prowl around there—the shops with the Cuban sausages and that tar-black coffee, the old dons clicking the dominoes like castanets in their clubs, the narrow, old-world streets where the apartments above the shops have those iron-filigree balconies projecting over the sidewalk. Is your place an apartment like that?''

"Yes. The rent is pretty modest in those old buildings.''

"I guess it's not like New Orleans, where a place in the French Quarter would cost an arm and a leg."

"Not hardly," Andrea agreed.

Mom glanced up at the young brunette waitress who had approached their booth. "Jess," Mom asked, "what are you folks gonna have?"

The waitress's eyes grew round. "Well, cook my hominy" she gasped. "As I live and breath, if it ain't Jess Clark in the flesh!"

"Hush your mouth, girl," Mom snapped. "He and the lady came in to eat as quiet-like as possible. You want to stir up everybody in the place? Why do you think I sat them in this booth where they wouldn't be seen?"

"I'm sorry." The waitress glanced around guiltily. But

her words had gone unnoticed. The place continued its rough-hewn, pleasantly noisy way. She looked back at Jess. "Your secret is safe, if you'll autograph that menu for me. Geez, the menu from which I served Jess Clark!"

Jess smiled pleasantly and nodded. Andrea caught herself relaxing after a moment of suspense. She realized that being in public with him created its own mild tension.

She supposed there must be times when he had to smile and wave even if he didn't feel like it. And there must be times, too, when he was at actual physical risk, with security guards trying to hustle him through a mob where fans reached out to tear at his clothing for souvenirs.

For herself, Andrea was uncomfortable in such limelight.

"How's the beef stew today, Mom?" Jess was asking.

"Super. Cook musta knowed you was coming!"

"That okay, Andrea?"

She nodded and the waitress left to fill the orders.

It was a lunch such as Andrea had never before experienced and would not easily forget. All about her was a cross section of people struggling to reach the bottom rung, starry-eyed youngsters contrasting with the sad images of morose has-beens sitting at the bar.

The meal was a hearty combination of tasty country-plain stew and corn muffins. As they ate, Jess and Mom talked about the old days when he'd worked as a part-time bouncer for her to pay for his grub while scrounging music gigs.

Andrea learned that Mom had a shoebox behind the bar filled with unpaid tabs and bad checks. Most who had put slips there forgot about them. But there were exceptions that shored up Mom's incurably optimistic faith in human

"Who is she, Jess?"

"Not fair, Jess, keeping us sweating on the rumor that the latest heartthrob has flown in from out of town."

"Miss, how did you meet?"

"Are you a model for one of the big agencies?"

"What is your impression of Nashville, gorgeous?"

"This way, please. Look in this direction." Electronic flashes winked.

The unblinking eye of the TV camera stared at her.

"Hold it!" Jess boomed in a voice that brooked no challenge. The crowd from Mom's had spilled out, making a jostling addition to the disorderly mass.

Jess held them in command long enough to make a statement.

"The lady's name is Andrea Castille. She is from Tampa, Florida. She's an executive at the factory of Castille Guitars, makers of fine instruments. . . ."

A sharp-faced woman said pleasantly, "She looks more like a movie star, the classic dark beauty of Hedy Lamarr, Liz Taylor. . . ."

"Why, thank you, Miss Birdsong, I couldn't agree more," Jess said, raising his hat as he bowed.

A hollow-chested, middle-aged reporter stopped them. "Are you adding to your business conglomerate, Jess? Buying a guitar factory this time?"

Jess avoided a direct answer. "Maybe," he hedged. "We're still negotiating."

"With your endorsement they'd better add an assembly line," a cocky young reporter exclaimed. "How did the deal come about? How much are they paying you? Will you be doing TV spots?"

"The deal hasn't been finalized," Jess said, "which is why Miss Castille is here. What you see, folks, is what it is. Nothing up our sleeves."

"Strictly business, Jess?" the owner of a wiseacre voice asked cynically.

"No further comment," Jess said, running out of patience. "When there is something real to report, my public relations people will arrange a news conference."

He had maneuvered them so that a smiling, hand-waving escape was possible. He and Andrea scrambled into his car and then he honked his way through the small traffic jam that had filled the street in front of Mom's place.

They didn't speak until they were several blocks away, safely lost in traffic.

"Sorry, Andrea. But that's the way the ball bounces. Have to be as tolerant as we can. They're just people trying to make a living like the rest of us."

"Who were they, Jess? I mean, I know they were media, but were they the tabloid variety?"

"Celebrity gossip? I'm afraid most them were, Andrea. Local newspaper columnists and photographers who fill their own space and then try to pick up a little extra bread by working as stringers for one of the national rags that sensationalize rumors about celebrities."

"Oh, my," she murmured, her cheeks growing warm at the thought of a photograph of her beside Jess and the lurid gossip that would accompany the picture.

"I'm afraid we might run into that sort of thing wherever we go. How would you like to take a spin out to Skyland for a little peace and quiet?"

Skyland. That would be his private sanctuary. She had

read about it in the press releases and magazine stories about Jess Clark. It was the kind of small, secluded ranch so many Nashville celebrities owned outside the city. Their own version of the country life they sang about. A place like the home of Hooter and Marilee, with a swimming pool, landing strip and horse stables.

She felt she had no business going to a secluded setting like that with Jess, alone.

"Ever go horseback riding?" he asked.

"Yes, I love it," she replied, weakening.

"I've got a little filly that I bet you'd just love. There's a nice ride along the river, lots of trees, pretty scenery, wildflowers. It's quiet out there. The city seems a million miles away."

"It sounds heavenly."

He smiled, taking that for his answer, and swung his car sharply to the right at the next intersection.

Andrea felt the beat of her heart accelerate. She had the feeling that the next few hours were going to change her life forever. But she was beyond stopping the rushing events that had caught her in their current. Nor did she want to. There was no more use in analyzing, in searching for answers to her emotions. Right or wrong, she knew the answer now.

The answer was as simple and old as the heartbeat of the human experience.

She had fallen in love with Jess Clark.

It was insanity. It was dangerous, it was self-destructive. Jess had given not one hint that he was interested in her for anything more than a passing romantic adventure.

But reason had failed her. She was overwhelmed by a

flood of emotion greater than anything she had ever before experienced. She only thought of the present, of being with Jess, of holding him close to her breast. This tender glow suffused her entire being and shook her to her soul.

Her voice was thick with the feelings surging through her. "Better stop by the hotel so I can pick up something suitable to wear on a horse if we're going riding."

"Sure. Do you have a pair of blue jeans along?"

"I think I just happened to have packed a pair."

She settled back, her gaze stealing to his profile, to his strong hands on the wheels, hands that could be tender, hands that could caress her body with a touch that set her flesh on fire.

She closed her eyes. She felt intoxicated.

Chapter Ten

$\mathcal{H}$er emotions were in such turmoil that the rushing scene about her hardly impinged on her attention. Under different circumstances she would have enjoyed the wind on her cheek, the comfortably lazy blue summer sky, the prosperous countryside, the sight of a pair of colts cavorting in a green pasture.

But the inner tumult was more real than anything else. Her very being was divided, the parts clashing in painful conflict. How was it possible to feel so many things for a man all at once? To feel fright in his presence, but a fright that was delicious. To want to draw away from him, but have his strong arms reach out and pull her back. The mundane world slipped away in the fantasies of a pair of lips coming closer to her with a promise of fire while his hands sought the warm, intimate places of her body. . . .

She had never felt this way before—exhilarated, despairing, wildly defensive and turgidly wanton. What had happened to her? She was a proper and well-bred drawing room lady.

The car had slowed, turned. The objective world shifted back into focus. They had finally reached the outer perimeters of Skyland. She'd glimpsed a No Trespassing sign when he'd turned from the main highway to a private road.

Her impression was one of simplicity, peacefulness. The fences were ordinary split-rail. The gently rising and falling terrain was soothingly bucolic. Tall pines, hoary oaks, the shadows of a cool, green glen. A breeze wafted the sage of a meadow. A sleek chestnut mare contentedly grazed on a stretch of pastureland while her foal nursed.

No impressive formal gardens. No mansion on a hilltop. Nothing visible to suggest that this was the abode of a millionaire. He had left it all as unscarred as possible, as if he were in rapport with the earth and was unwilling to have bulldozers tear at its vitals. She was sure all the modern accoutrements were there, the normal conveniences. For him, the necessities would include electronic surveillance and probably the computerization of functional details. But all that was hidden. Even the power lines had been buried and sodded over, healing the wounds of the earth.

The house was a large structure of natural wood, its peaked gabled roof of cedar shingles. Its arched, leaded windows winked friendly invitations as they caught glints from the shafts of light and shadows filtering through the surrounding trees. The lodge gave the impression of having been born of the earth itself rather than on the drafting table of a gifted architect.

He stopped near the house and turned to her. "Well?" he asked.

She drew a deep breath, drinking in the perfume of leaves and grass and wildflowers. "It's not just beautiful." She sighed. "It's perfection."

His smile broadened. He started the car again, drove around back and parked in front of a long, open-fronted shed that sheltered a station wagon, a tractor and a battered Jeep such as a working farmer might use.

She was glad to be getting out of the car, catching a breath, standing upright. They walked around to the front of the house, across a rambling gallery. He opened the front door.

The interior exuded a sense of quiet comfort—a cathedral ceiling, hewn rafters with wood grain like satin, a huge stone fireplace, hooked rugs, big couches and chairs done in wood and soft brocades.

Only the wall centered by the fireplace revealed that this was the abode of a celebrity. The expanse of wall all around the fireplace was an area of hand-rubbed natural-wood shelving and framings displaying gold records, trophies, award plaques—visible evidence of his fantastic achievements in the entertainment world.

It was the only concession to his professional life. Everything else about the place suggested ownership by a well-to-do farmer or rancher.

He showed her to a room where she could change. Then they went outside to a corral, where he saddled horses. She fell in love with Sunrise, the filly he had picked out for her to ride. The horse was just spirited enough to challenge her riding ability.

The ride was breathtaking, a trail along the river under

giant trees, across creek beds of pure white gravel, along banks of ferns and river flowers. Squirrels chattered and played above them in the branches and birds sang.

The shadows were lengthening when at last they returned to the house. Andrea felt drenched with the beauty of nature. She tried to put into words her reaction to the scenery but failed. "I guess I'd have to be a poet to describe it," she said as they dismounted. "Maybe you could put it all in a song sometime."

"I've tried. So far, I haven't been able to do it justice," he admitted.

In the house, she went to the room where she had changed. Her dress was on the bed where she had left it. She slipped out of her shirt with slow, languorous movements. She felt the brush of fabric against her bare legs as she stepped out of her jeans. She dawdled like a child. Out here, she felt as if she had escaped the prison of time.

A sound in the doorway caused her to spin around. She gasped and snatched up her dress to cover her.

Jess was leaning against the doorjamb holding a drink in each hand, a lazy, good-natured smile on his lips.

"You might have knocked," she chided softly.

"But think of the scenery I would have missed—a lot more beautiful than the river bank."

"Jess! Please don't embarrass me!"

He raised an eyebrow. "Why? Because I happened to catch a glimpse of you in your underwear? Heck, there was a lot more showing when you were in that red bikini the other night."

"That's different!"

He shrugged. "I don't know why." He lingered a bit longer, his eyes growing smoky as his gaze drifted over what the dress she was clutching to her bosom failed to cover. Mingled with her embarrassment, she was conscious of a rising heat within her, a stirring of her womanhood, responding to the desire the sight of her could awaken in a man. His maleness delighted in seeing her like this; her femaleness felt a muffled excitement at being seen.

"You have beautiful legs, Andrea—long, slender, smooth. A slim waist, nice, full breasts. The good Lord sure blessed you with more than the usual share of womanly gifts." He sounded almost humble.

"Well, thank you, Jess," she said, her cheeks coloring. "Just the same, you are embarrassing me. So would you be a good boy and go away so I can put my dress on?"

He gave her that lean, crooked grin again. "Sure."

He left. She slipped into her dress, savoring the caress of the soft fabric against her skin. All of her senses were heightened. Through an open window, she could hear the clear, brilliant song of a bird and catch the perfume of wildflowers.

A few minutes later, she entered the living area. Jess was comfortably seated on the couch, sipping his drink. He rose quickly and made a gesture that invited her to join him on the couch.

"This drink is my own recipe," he said, offering her a glass when she was seated. "Tell me what you think."

She took a sip, tasting the tangy, sweet moisture on the tip of her tongue, then letting it trickle down her throat. "Ummm. Delicious. What does it have in it?"

"Different kinds of fruit juices, some crushed mint, a dash of gin. Real polite summer drink. I promise it won't bowl you over like Hooter's punch."

"That was pretty potent stuff," she agreed.

He took his seat on the couch. She curled her legs under her, facing him. They were so close she thought she could feel the heat of his body. The couch formed a comfortable cradle for the curves of her body. Pillows were soft against her back. Except for the faint, steady ticking of an old-fashioned clock on the mantel, the room was silent. If he had caretakers, they must have been given the day off. She felt totally isolated here with him. The implication of their intimacy in this house alone together with the bedrooms but a short distance away down the hall made her blood course in a thickened, rushing stream.

It seemed inevitable that he was going to kiss her.

She said, her voice a trifle unsteady, "Jess, would you sing that song for me, the one on your new album about a lovin' song."

He smiled in surprise. " 'Sing Me a Lovin' Song'? You heard it? I didn't think this was your kind of music."

"Well, I guess I didn't, either. I still don't. But when I was in Tampa, I heard the song in a record shop. I—I bought the album," she confessed. "It—it's quite lovely the way you sing it."

He looked pleased. "Okay. If you'll do one thing for me?"

"What's that?" she asked warily.

"I wonder if you'd let your hair fall down loose. Not many women these days have waist-length hair."

She smiled, somehow flattered. "All right."

She reached up and slipped the pins from her hair. She

ran her fingers through the gleaming thick strands, suddenly grateful that nature had blessed her with such a luxurious mane. She shook it out and let it fall in a silken black stream down her back. It was almost like undressing before him. She felt her breathing become slow and deep.

Jess stared at her. "Beautiful," he murmured. "If you want my opinion, women gave up something when they started cutting their hair short. There's something awfully loose and sexy about a woman letting her hair down that way. Seems to me a woman would look twice as naked if she had long hair falling down her bare back."

"Now you're embarrassing me again!"

"Can't blame a guy for dreaming."

The way he was looking at her, she knew he was imagining her exactly that way, without a stitch on, as her hair cascaded down her back. Her heart responded with a quickened rhythm that she could hear pulsing in her ears. The look in his eyes made her acutely self-conscious while at the same time sending a pleasant tingling sensation down her spine. She felt warm all over.

She tried to break the tension that was building between them like the throbbing of primitive jungle drums. The pulse in her throat was growing more rapid. "You promised to sing," she reminded him softly in a voice that had become thickened with the emotions churning in her.

"Yes, so I did. You let your hair fall down for me. I reckon the least I can do is sing for you."

He reached for a guitar that was propped behind the couch. He touched the strings, turning a fret until he was satisfied it was in tune.

He struck a full chord and in his rich voice began singing. It was the same soft, intimate style she'd heard on the record. It had the quality of a lover tenderly murmuring in the ear of his wife or mistress whose tousled head rested on the pillow beside his as they held hands, listening to the strains of a 'lovin' song' from a jukebox downstairs, across the street.

But now it was no impersonal, electronically reproduced voice on a record. It was Jess, here, singing the song for her alone.

His voice resonated deeply within her, touching responses that were almost unbearably delicious. It seemed to envelop her, caress her, speak to her innermost feelings, awaken poignant emotions. She closed her eyes. Her breasts were rising and falling in measured rhythm to the emotions he had stirred in her. Her heart thudded with the pulsing beat of the lovers' cadence.

She wanted the song to go on forever, but it ended, leaving her in its spell. He put the guitar down and took her in his arms.

"Oh, Jess. . . ." she whispered.

He was gazing directly into her eyes, touching something so deep and personal that she quivered. It was as if he could see into her very soul. She was powerless in the grip of that hypnotic gaze. Their eyes drank deeply from the essence of the other. Time had lost all meaning.

She was vaguely aware of his masculine smells, the faint aroma of horse leather, a spicy after-shave lotion, a kind of male musk. He was so close she could feel his breath on her cheek. Slowly, ever so slowly, his lips moved closer to hers. With his mouth against hers, he whispered her name once.

His lips claimed hers.

Her arms went around him. Her body had grown limp

with surrender, molding her soft curves to the hard, masculine contours of his body.

His kisses ranged down her cheek to the hollow of her throat. He stroked her hair and then gently opened the fastening on the back of her dress so that it fell away from her shoulder. She gasped softly, her eyes closed, as his kisses found the hollow under her collarbone, bringing goose bumps to the tender, willing flesh.

Her breathing had become labored. The earth seemed to be spinning away. As if in a dream, she was aware of his lips seeking to know her more intimately, finding the delicate, intimate hollow between her breasts.

Then his shirt parted. She felt a shock as her breasts were mashed against the masculine pressure of the hair and muscle of his bared chest.

"Jess . . . Jess. . . ." she moaned.

His hands, trembling now, slid the hem of her dress up, and she felt the touch of his hands caressing her thighs, making her flesh quiver, igniting flames that raged through her innermost being.

Time and reason were blotted out in mounting waves of desire. Passion brought incoherent exclamations from her lips. She quivered from his touch. His lips were setting her on fire.

He was a skillful lover. He knew how to tempt, how to offer, then hold back, how to give pleasure, to hint at ecstasy until she was turned into a panting, clinging slave.

She didn't want to think about other arms that had taught him those skills. She existed only for this moment. Every molecule of her being was alive. Sensation after sensation washed over her in ecstatic waves. Her blood was on fire. Her nerves tingled like high wires in an electrical storm. Her flesh, pliant and yielding, was hot to the touch.

Her inhibitions were swept away; she felt abandoned.

Suddenly, through the raging storm of the primitive passion that had wiped out all her reason and restraint, there came a shattering crash.

Jess came upright with a jerk.

Numbly clasping her disarranged clothing to her bosom, Andrea sat up. "What in heaven's name was that?"

"Don't know," Jess mumbled, stuffing his shirt back in place.

"It sounded like a tree falling on the house!"

"More like a car running into something. Come on." Jess hurried to the door.

Andrea rose, disheveled. She finished adjusting her dress, trying to gather her shocked senses. She felt weak. Her legs trembled. The shock had been like a dash of cold water. She was like a sleepwalker, half-dazed, reluctant to exchange the dream for the harsh shape of reality.

Sobered, steadied, strength returning, her mind flashed to the event that had intruded. Something about it awoke a feeling of dread. She was sure there had been an accident of some kind.

When she reached the front gallery, she saw that her surmise had been correct. A neat little hatchback had left the road leading to the house. It no longer looked so neat. It was sitting lopsided and askew at the edge of the driveway near the oak tree, which now had deep gashes in its bark. The car's bumper had been turned into a curled pretzel of chrome, the left headlight a vacant eye socket staring in the wrong direction from a crumpled fender. Dust all the length of the road, a plume of dust was slowly dissipating in the breeze, attesting to the speed with which the car had been moving before skidding off the road.

Jess was beside the car, pulling the driver's door open, helping the petite blond driver from under the steering wheel.

Nori Lawrence had obviously rounded a bend in the driveway at too high a speed and sideswiped a huge granddaddy of an oak tree, leaving a great yellowish-white scar on the tree trunk.

Andrea hurried from the front gallery and ran toward them. Nori appeared dazed but mobile, holding on to Jess's arm to steady herself and taking the first tentative step toward the house. She had a small cut on her forehead, which oozed blood.

Andrea reached their side, breathless. Surprisingly, except for the minor gash, Nori seemed unharmed beyond the aftermath of surprise and shock. Dressed in jeans, knit shirt, huaraches, she merely looked rumpled. But that could have been as much from her drinking as from the accident; she smelled like a brewery.

Nori looked at the car, then tried to focus her eyes on Jess and Andrea. She giggled. "Some mess, huh?"

Jess scowled. "Nori, you're drunk."

"So what else's new?"

"You promised me you weren't going to pull something like this. You gave me your word you were going to stay away from the sauce."

Tears filled her eyes. "Please don't be mad at me, Jess honey. Can't stand it when you're mad. . . ."

"Well, I am mad. A lot of people have gone way out on a limb to give you this recording shot tomorrow, and you pull something like this. How are you going to sound, all hungover?"

She swayed, hair tumbling over one eye. "Be all right, Jess. Promise." She started crying. "Got scared, honey. Got to thinkin' 'bout it . . . wonderin' if I still have it. What if I blow it? Just had a little drink to steady my nerves."

"You had a lot more than a little drink. More like a bottle."

She pouted. "Okay, more like a bottle." She gave him a defiant look.

Jess glanced at Andrea. "She has an important recording date scheduled for tomorrow," he explained. "It could mean a second chance for her, a comeback."

Nori said, "Hey, maybe there's one more drink in th' bottle. Don' want to let it go to waste. Waste not, want not." She made a lurching turn in the direction of the car. Jess gripped her slender arm above the elbow and firmly turned her back toward the house.

"No way, Nori. It's into the house and some black coffee for you."

"No," she said with a pout.

"Nori, for heaven's sake," Jess swore in exasperation.

Andrea wondered if he had been through this Nori scene before, perhaps many times before. And yet . . . he'd never put a stop to them. When she was in trouble, she seemed to head straight for Jess. Perhaps, Andrea thought with a sudden cold wrench deep inside, the blond pixie appealed to him. She was cuddly, apparently dependent on him. Is that what he needed in a woman?

What was their relationship, anyway? Andrea wondered, feeling suddenly cold and alone.

Tears spilled from Nori's eyes. Her cute little head fell against his shoulder. "But you'll be there with me, in the house? I couldn't stand bein' alone in that great big house with all this emptiness inside me, Jess."

"Sure, Andrea and I will be there," Jess said comfortingly, slipping a supporting arm about Nori's shoulder and walking her to the door.

Andrea felt like the odd wheel as she followed. Jess opened the door and practically scooped Nori inside.

"Tell you what, Andrea. See if you can get Nori into bed. Second room on the right down the hall. I'll go make a pot of black coffee."

It took some coaxing, but Andrea managed to get Nori into the bedroom. Once there, the small blonde collapsed on the bed, the wind out of her sails. She meekly allowed Andrea to help her undress. Then she crawled beneath the covers. She looked at Andrea sullenly.

"You been out here with Jess all day, huh?"

"Part of the day. We went riding."

"I'll bet," said the blond singer, her eyes damp with tears again. "I knew Jess was going to score with you."

"Nori—"

"Oh, don't look shocked." Her eyes looked defiant. "I don't care. Jess is all man. You're somebody different from the usual crowd. You're beautiful and you got class. Not the kind of class Jess's used to. So he wanted you and he got you." She shrugged. "It doesn't matter. He's scored. Big deal for his ego. Down inside, he's runnin' scared like the rest of us. Got to keep provin' himself. Now that he's had you, he'll toss you aside and come back to me. I'm his woman. Always have been . . . alway will be. I'm the one who really counts to Jess. You'll see. . . ."

Her words became incoherent and she drifted into a sodden sleep.

Andrea stood beside the bed, frozen with shock. Was there any truth to Nori's words, or was it the rambling of a scared, lost little soul?

She looked down at the pixie face with fingers curled near her cheek, and touseled blond hair. Asleep she looked innocent, almost childlike, the lines of dissipation softened.

It was not hard to imagine Jess in love with her. She was a cute little thing. And unlike Andrea, she came from Jess's world. She fitted into the honky-tonks, the beer joints, the one-night stands. She talked their language, lived their music. Wasn't there some kind of country-western song about a honky-tonk angel? That was an apt description. Nori was a honky-tonk angel, familiar to Jess's frame of reference. Andrea and Jess were from totally different worlds, utter strangers brought together by an explosive primitive attraction she couldn't begin to understand.

Andrea sighed, gathered up the young woman's discarded clothing and opened a closet door in search of a hanger. She froze, staring at the garments there. The blood drained from her face. The woman's clothes, judging by the size and style, could belong to no one but Nori.

Nori was quite at home here at Jess Clark's Skyland.

Chapter Eleven

Andrea woke up with a throbbing headache. The tears with which she had soaked her pillow last night were no doubt the cause.

After Nori had fallen asleep, Andrea had gone to Jess and asked to be taken back to the hotel. She'd tried to keep a lid on her feelings, but she supposed it had been obvious to him she was disturbed. He'd probably thought it was because of the interruption of their romantic encounter and the intrusion of Nori Lawrence into their isolation. She'd made no effort to clear up that misconception. All she had left after today was a small shred of pride and that, at least, she planned to hold on to. It was the memory she wanted to forget.

When they were back in Nashville, approaching the hotel, Jess said, "I'm sorry about Nori messing things up for us that way. But we still have the rest of the evening. We could go out to dinner, then have some time together alone. . . .''

The meaning was obvious. After a romantic dinner to reestablish the mood, he would come up to her hotel room. They could resume where they had left off when Nori crashed into the tree, this time continuing on to the logical completion of their lovemaking.

Earlier in the evening Andrea would have been willing, but that was no longer the case. Discovering that Nori was living with Jess had in one shocking moment changed everything. Andrea was in love with Jess. That was something that could not be changed. But how could she give herself to him under the circumstances, knowing that he was already involved with Nori?

What she felt most was disillusionment. She had overcome her initial distrust of Jess, had turned him into a hero. And now she'd found out her first suspicions had been right on target. All Jess wanted out of her was a conquest, thinking that Andrea's body was a bit of largess added to the terms of the endorsement contract.

She should be furious with him, but she wasn't. No one could blame a jungle cat for stalking its prey. That was an ingrained instinct in the animal. And Jess Clark was a predatory animal.

No, it was Andrea Castille who deserved the blame for falling into the trap so blindly, so willingly. Jess cared nothing for her as a person. When had he once mentioned the word *love?* Never! He hadn't even given her the usual line about how much he cared for her, more than any other woman he had ever known. At least give him credit for that. He hadn't handed her any lies or raised false hopes about a commitment beyond that moment of passion. All he had done was to go around being Jess Clark, oozing that irresistible magnetism and charisma, sing her one love song, and she'd been totally mesmerized, ready to fall into his bed.

What she now felt was mostly sadness and a dreadful sense of betrayal and loss. In a few days Jess had taught her the real meaning of love, a willingness to become totally committed to a man. Her life had taken on a whole new meaning, like a diamond that had been cut and was now shining brilliantly. Then, in one heartbreaking moment, all that had been swept away, leaving her to feel like a helpless child alone in a dense forest, completely lost.

She tried to console herself with the thought that she wasn't the first woman to make a fool of herself over a man. And she wouldn't be the last!

Then she thought about poor little Nori, loyal to a man like Jess Clark. Nori was the real victim. Why was it that men like Jess often had that kind of woman, desperately hanging on, enduring one humiliation after another? Was it a form of masochism?

Now Jess was pressing her for an answer to his suggestion for the evening. She made a determined effort to marshal her thoughts. Her first instinct was to tell him off, send him packing, giving it to him straight about what a rat she thought he was.

But how could she? No matter how much she might hate him, he had done something to her life that would forever make it different. The bittersweet memories were there to stay.

With an effort, she smiled. "Jess, forgive me, but I don't feel up to dinner this evening. I'm tired and I'm getting a headache. Would you mind terribly just dropping me off at the hotel?''

He frowned. ''Sure wish I could change your mind,'' he said slowly.

''Another time,'' she said despite a lump in her throat. She touched his hand briefly, then fought back the tears that the momentary contact brought. It was like a gesture of farewell.

''Well, okay,'' he said reluctantly. ''Boy, I could strangle Nori.''

I'll bet you could, she thought.

''But I'll see you tomorrow, right?'' he asked.

''Yes—all . . . all right.''

''Have you ever been to a recording session in a big-time professional studio?''

''No.''

''Well, I want you to be there tomorrow when Nori cuts that master. We're going to back up Nori's vocal. I think you'll find it interesting.''

''All right,'' she agreed, wondering how she would find the strength to be there. Maybe she could think up some kind of excuse.

When he stopped at the hotel, she forced herself to permit him to kiss her good night. Then she fled to her room where she cried herself to sleep. . . .

Now Andrea wondered if she would ever feel like getting out of bed again.

The buzz of her telephone put an end to thoughts of pulling the cover over her head and hiding from life.

She looked at it with dread. She was sure it was Jess and

she didn't want to answer it. But it could be a call from Tampa, something about her grandfather.

Dragging herself out of the depths of her depression, she reached for the instrument.

"Miss Castille?" a woman's brisk, businesslike voice asked.

"Yes."

"This is the office of Randy Davis, Mr. Jess Clark's business manager."

"Oh, yes," Andrea said, suddenly coming wide-awake.

"Mr. Davis got back to Nashville late last night. He's had a message from Mr. Clark to put you at the head of his appointment calendar first thing today."

At last! Andrea was elated. "Yes, fine. I'm very anxious to talk with Mr. Davis. When does he want to see me?"

"Well, this morning, if that's convenient with you."

Andrea shot a quick look at her watch. "Certainly. I could be there in an hour."

"All right. We'll be expecting you." Then she gave directions to the office.

Andrea hung up and flew into action. She dashed into the shower, then selected a businesslike navy suit. She pinned up her hair in a severe bun. She grabbed up the briefcase with the contracts and made a stop at the coffee shop for a cup of black coffee. Then she had the hotel doorman secure a cab for her.

She was in Randy Davis's office exactly an hour from the time she'd concluded the phone conversation with his secretary.

The offices of Jess's business manager were what she'd

expected—plush, elegant, deep pile carpeting, rich paneling, leather upholstered furnishing, polished mahogany desks. In the outer office, three secretaries were busy with files and computers.

Davis himself was something of a surprise. She'd expected a middle-aged man with graying temples, sharp blue eyes and the demeanor of a corporate lawyer. But Randy Davis was a few years younger than Jess. He had a mop of unruly brown hair. When they talked, he leaned back in his swivel chair, crossed his western boots on his desk and shoved rimless glasses up into his hair. Only his eyes fit her preconceived image. They were blue, bright as marbles and piercingly sharp.

"Jess wanted me to apologize for this delay," he said in a soft Carolina drawl. "I guess he explained about the problem that had me tied up out on the West Coast."

"Yes, I know about that." Andrea nodded. "What I've been more concerned about is Mr. Clark's sudden change of heart about our agreement. I came to Nashville thinking this deal was firmed up and just required the final signing of the contracts. Now he's come up with an entirely new proposition—one that is totally unacceptable to us."

"You mean his idea of a partnership?"

"Exactly. Did you know about this?"

"No ma'am, to tell the truth, I didn't. I'm like you. I thought we had the deal all settled before I left for California. Looks like Jess got to thinking about it and came up with a whole new set of ideas. He briefed me on it late last night when I got back into town."

"Mr. Davis, the manufacture of Castille guitars has been exclusively a family enterprise for generations. I know my grandfather would never agree to this kind of partnership.''

''Well, there would be a lot of benefits for your grandfather. Y'see, Jess has in mind going a lot farther than just doing some promotional advertising. As he explained it to me, he wants to put the weight of his whole organization behind Castille Guitars and that includes investing capital if necessary.''

''I appreciate all that. Our plant manager agreed that such a partnership could perhaps be to our advantage. But none of you seems to understand the human element involved. I tried to explain to Jess that in my grandfather's eyes, by building Castille guitars he is carrying on a family tradition handed down from one generation to the next. It has always been an exclusive family business. He simply would not consider a partnership. He'd let the business go under first. . . .''

Davis frowned, chewing on his bottom lip. ''I was hoping you might be able to persuade him. Jess has his heart set on this partnership.''

Andrea's eyes filled with tears. ''Mr. Davis, I'm appealing to you and to Mr. Clark. My grandfather is not well. He's in the hospital back in Tampa now, recovering from a heart attack that his doctor thinks has been brought on by business worries. If you'd get Jess to sign the original agreement I brought with me, it would be the best medicine in the world for him. You have no idea how he's counting on it. You know our terms are fair. We've made Jess Clark a more than generous offer. If he turns it down now because of his stubborn notion about this impossible partnership, it would be a crushing blow to my grandfather.''

Clark's business manager grinned. "Jess is plenty stubborn. I agree with you about that, Miss Castille. Generally, he leaves most business matters up to me. Once in a while, though, he digs his heels in about something and a Missouri mule can't budge him. However, I'll talk to him some more and see what we can come up with. Apparently your grandfather is just as stubborn as Jess."

"You can be sure of that," Andrea said. "Either Jess Clark will have to agree to our original proposition or I'll be forced to go back and tell grandfather that the deal is off and that means the end of Castille Guitars."

Davis shook his head. "None of us wants to see that happen. I can't promise anything, but I'll have another talk with Jess and we'll get back to you. Okay?"

Andrea nodded. She gathered up her purse and rose.

Davis said, "Either Jess or I will get in touch with you. I think he's planning to take you to a recording session this afternoon, right?"

"Yes." Andrea made one final tearful appeal. "If you have any influence with him, please try to get him to relent and sign these contracts." She placed the papers on his desk.

"As I said before, I won't promise anything, Miss Castille. The bottom line is that I only work for Jess. He's still the boss around here. But I'll make it clear that there's no use trying to talk your grandfather into a partnership. It'll be up to him to decide how to take it from there."

She returned to her hotel room. Shortly before noon the phone rang. It was Jess's voice she heard, wringing a fresh twist of pain. He sounded cheerful. "Wanted to remind you about the recording date this afternoon. You haven't forgotten about it, have you?"

"I remember," she said, trying to bring some kind of lift to her voice.

"Great. I'll pick you up right after lunch and we'll go to the studio together."

She wanted desperately to ask him if he'd talked with his business manager, if he'd made a decision about the contracts, but her nerve failed her. She'd have to wait until he brought up the matter.

Under other circumstances she would be excited at the privilege of seeing a big-time Nashville recording being made. The situation being what it was, it was going to be an ordeal she must somehow get through.

Jess seemed oblivious to her state of mind. He sounded cheerful, high, excited. Well, why not? Somehow he had wrangled a chance for his mistress, Nori, to make a comeback. This was her big day.

Andrea was impressed by the name on the studio office. It was one of the biggest record companies in Nashville. Nori's comeback was certainly being backed by a prestigious label.

Jess introduced her to some of the executives, then took her to a soundproofed observation room which gave a view through a glass wall of the studio area where the actual performance and recording took place. There he introduced her to Corliss Jones, who held some kind of executive position in the department of marketing research.

"Sorry to desert you, Andrea, but they need me down there. Corliss can fill you in on anything you want to know. See you after we finish cutting the tape."

Corliss was a tall, angular woman with a pleasant smile.

She had a long, narrow face and big, square teeth, a gangling and awkward figure in a simple gray suit. By all rights she was an unattractive woman, but her warm smile and the friendly expression in her large gray eyes softened the angularity.

Andrea sensed a mood of tension in the observation room. The four rows of plush theater-type seats were partially filled by men and women who, Andrea surmised, were company people. The talk was low-pitched, casual shop talk and gossip perhaps to relieve the tension as they stared through the plate glass at the recording studio where musicians and technicians were milling about, discussing microphone setup, tuning instruments. Andrea saw Jess's people and offered a wave of her hand. Marilee saw her first and spoke to the others. Peewee, Hooter and Skeeter signaled brief greetings. Jess and Nori weren't in evidence.

"Well, I've got my fingers crossed that it goes well," Corliss said. "I hope Nori didn't duck in a bar for a last-minute bracer."

Andrea was aware of a note of quiet concern in the other woman's voice. "Are you a close friend of Nori's?"

"I know her fairly well. She has a quality about her—like everybody's kid sister. I'm hoping she'll pull this off. The kid has had a rough time of it."

Kid sister? The pixie wanton who got drunk, smashed up a car, then made everything right by tumbling into Jess Clark's bed? Andrea wasn't sure if she'd agree with the analogy.

"Of course," Corliss added, "I have my selfish business reasons for wanting this to be a hit record. It never hurts the company to hit the top forty with a new release.''

''How did today's recording session come about?''

''There's this guy, Casey Millbanks—love Casey, feel at home with him, he's so gosh-darned gawky and stringbean like myself. Well, he finally got his act together. Casey was one of those impoverished young newcomers among the ranks of hopeful producers. He did a couple of cuts that were actually very good but somehow didn't hit the charts. He couldn't get the right distribution and PR doors open and DJs to air his platters. He was despairing of ever making it, then he gloomed the idea of a Nori Lawrence comeback. With her one big gold-record hit and the lesser successes in the past, she was the biggest name available to Casey for a last shot. Casey went to Jess Clark with the idea. Jess swings a lot of weight in Nashville, as you know. There's more than a dollar or two of Jess Clark's money at risk right now in this studio. And Jess offered his group as a backup. Who can top a combination like that? I hope Nori realizes how rich she is in friends if she makes it this go-round.''

The man sitting in front of Andrea leaned forward and flipped a switch on a console. Immediately all the sounds from the recording room poured through speakers into the observation booth.

There was a babble of complaints, instructions, murmurs of approval among technicians, some of whom were visible behind other glass walls at consoles in the control room on the far side of the studio. Sound technicians were moving about among the musicians and instruments and maze of cables that seemed to be everywhere. Bulging headphones trailing thick black wires appeared to be standard gear for the technicians.

"Ed, number one mike has a rasp. . . ."

"No, damn it! The direction on number three—Skeeter will you please leave the blasted chair in place!"

"Hooter, it's all brushwork on the snare at letter *B*. Right . . . okay, I've got a sound level. . . ."

Corliss explained to Andrea, "If it all sounds confusing, it really isn't. They're a finicky bunch. Every mike, every intonation has to be exactly right. I hope we're not in for too many takes. Getting five minutes off can sometimes kill the better part of a day, and we're getting started after lunch. Each musician, you see, will be recorded on a track. The microphone there beside the piano is waiting for Nori and the transcription of the voice track. We can do up to thirty-two separate tracks all at once in this particular studio. Tracks can be extracted so a musician can correct something in his single part, if the situation calls for it in the opinion of Warren Clive, the chief engineer. When everything is tracked, the mixdown, as it's called, takes place. This is the final electronic process in preparation of the master recording, the finalization of everything in stereophonic sound. From the master, the records, cassettes, eight-tracks will be mass-produced for, we hope, a million people flocking to the stores, record shops and mail-order clubs."

Any comments Andrea might have had were forgotten by the appearance of Jess and Nori in the far side of the recording area.

They entered through a door partly obscured from Andrea's line of sight by the location of the grand piano. Nori came in first, Jess close behind, his touch on her elbow. She paused there for a moment, like a diver on a very high board, taking a breath.

In the diminishing confusion due to Nori's appearance, Jess's voice came over the speakers, low and firm. "Do it!" he commanded.

As if the steel in his voice became a part of her, Nori's back straightened. Andrea was aware of a special look that passed between them. Nori appeared to draw strength from Jess's eyes. She moved quickly forward, around the piano, to the waiting microphone.

"I'm ready," she said quietly.

Jess had moved back through the entry and closed the door. A few seconds later Andrea saw him in the technicians' booth, leaning over a man sitting at a console, saying something to him.

A voice said, "All right, this is a—"

Skeeter coughed.

"Oh, great," the voice in the speaker said with a note of resignation. "Let's see if we can bust that little sound about eight bars in."

"Sorry," Skeeter said, shifting in his chair.

"Just don't cough on the take."

"I'm nervous," Skeeter said.

"Welcome to the club. We're all nervous."

"Look, I wrote this cotton-picking song. You'd be nervous, too, if it was your song."

"So I'm a no-talent technician."

"I didn't say that."

In a low voice, Andrea asked Corliss, "Is it usually this way?"

"It can be worse," Corliss said. "You should be around when a real donnybrook erupts between two characters sharing the affliction known as the prima donna complex. The language can get purple. I was here on one occasion when a soloist and an arranger started punching each other out. It was a real Saturday night free-for-all.'' She giggled. ''The arranger landed in the middle of a drum set. Smashed the base drum flat.''

''Okay,'' the technician's voice intoned from the speaker, ''if we can have the permission of Skeeter the skittish, it's a take. . . .''

An almost eerie silence settled in.

Then Peewee Sloan touched one of those sausage fingers to a piano key and a single tone came out, like a soft whisper in the night. While it held, another tone was added, then another and another until a full chord with a dark, dissonant note in the bass was hanging in a lonely, dark countryside, waiting for something to happen.

A counterpoint began to move rhythmically from the electric bass. Then a wire drum brush in Hooter's hand brought an insidious sizzle from a cymbal. A first tremulant, singing tone was drawn from Marilee's fiddle.

The intro built and then died, leaving only an echo. Then Nori's soft voice phrased the pickup notes to the chorus. Hers was the seeking voice of a simple country girl in a lonely farmhouse asking the question, ''Will memory return you to me?''

The lyrics Skeeter had written built a poignant cameo out of the theme and Nori gave it full expression. Not a muscle twitched in the observation booth. When the final note had died away, Corliss fell back, blinked a drop of moisture from her eyes and grinned at Andrea.

''Child, you've just heard it done the way the best of them are always trying to do it!''

Andrea nodded vaguely, staring through the glass wall at Nori. It was true, she had to admit to herself. It might not be her kind of music, but she knew she had just witnessed the expression of real talent.

Is that why Jess—

Because he knew what was there, beneath the booze and temper tantrums. . . .

But that bell-clear voice had sung, it seemed, more than just a song . . . had poured out the heart and soul of a betrayed woman . . . had reached down inside herself to tell of an actual experience. How else could the song have had such power? If so, who had betrayed her? Jess? Who else? Andrea thought with a deep, wrenching pain. As sorry as she felt for her own heartache, she felt as sorry for Nori. Andrea could go back to Tampa tomorrow and try to forget this kind of heartbreak. Poor little Nori was stuck with it.

Nori was the center of attention, compliments showered upon her, her face bright, suddenly years younger, happiness softening the ravages that had marred the gamine look.

But already the chief technician was criticizing, demanding a cessation of the small celebration taking place in the sound studio. "Cool it, you people. Back in places. Seconds mean money in here if you haven't heard. We've got work to do."

Corliss stirred, standing up. "That was the first run-through. For my money, we've got a top forty in the making. Now they'll start the retakes and I have places to be. I enjoyed meeting you, Andrea."

"Same here." Andrea rose and after a brief, parting handshake watched Corliss leave the observation booth.

Andrea turned to look across the sound studio, searching for Jess. She didn't see him. Then she turned, startled as a hand touched her shoulder.

"Hi," Jess said. "Well, what did you think? How did you like it?"

"It was quite an experience." She had to say honestly, "I've never heard a song more beautifully sung."

"It wasn't Schubert—not your kind of music," he pointed out in a mildly teasing tone."

"You're quite right, it wasn't. But I'm not a complete music snob. In the popular music field, it was outstanding."

"Yes, that it was," Jess agreed, gazing through the glass at Nori with an expression Andrea couldn't define. Half to himself, he said softly, "Don't blow it this time, kid. You're your own worse enemy. . . ."

He looked again at Andrea. "Let's go have a cup of coffee. I have something to tell you about the contracts."

The coffee shop was in the penthouse of the tall building. A perky waitress in a starched white apron seated them at the window comprising the eastern wall. The view across the Tennessee heartland was one of metro bustle, verdant fields, cloverleaves that turned into multilane highways swarming with truck and auto traffic looking like tiny bugs in the distance below.

"Andrea, would you like something to eat?"

"No, just a cup of coffee."

"That's fine for me, too," Jess told the waitress.

She left. Jess glanced idly out the window and made an observation about the view.

Andrea was on the edge of her chair. Her hands, hidden

by the table, were clasped in her lap. "Jess, you said you had something to tell me about the contracts."

He nodded. His gaze, serious and thoughtful, settled on her. "Randy called me after you'd been to his office this morning. He relayed your conversation with him. We spent the better part of an hour on the phone, hashing over this matter." He paused.

Andrea leaned tensely forward. "Well? What have you decided?" she demanded, her heart in her throat.

For an unbearably long moment, Jess just stared at her. Then he held up both hands in mock surrender. "I give up. I do believe you Castilles are the most stubborn family on the North American continent."

Andrea's heart gave a wild leap. "Oh, Jess, does that mean you're willing to give up the idea of a partnership and sign the original contracts?"

"Yeah." He nodded glumly.

Tears of joy spilled from Andrea's eyes. For the moment she completely forgot her own personal heartbreak. All she could think about was the joy that would fill her grandfather's eyes.

"Jess, I could kiss you!" she cried impulsively before she realized what she'd said.

His glum expression changed into a grin. "That'd be okay."

Then she remembered her personal situation with Jess and tempered her enthusiasm. "That's just an expression," she said. "But I do thank you, from the bottom of my heart, for Castille Guitars, for my grandfather . . . for all of us."

Jess gave her a searching, questioning look. Then he drew a breath and shrugged. "I guess you realize what you're passing up. Your grandfather's stubbornness is going to cost him a lot. He could have had me for free . . . in fact could have had my financial backing among other things."

"He'll get financial backing," she said confidently. "We have big things planned, using your endorsement in our promotion plans." Then she asked, "What made you change your mind?"

"Oh, several things. I certainly don't want to be responsible for making your grandfather have another heart attack. And I don't want to see Castille Guitars go down the tubes. The music world needs that kind of quality. And I could see that you weren't going to budge. It was what folks call a Mexican standoff. We were eyeball to eyeball and I finally blinked." He grinned. "You drive a hard bargain, little lady. Remind me never to get in a poker game with you!"

Then he added, "I thought you'd also want to know that Randy Davis said he's gone over the contracts with our attorney. Everything is in order. No problems. I'm stopping by his office in the morning to sign them."

The pent-up breath eased from Andrea's lungs. The weight of the world lifted from her shoulders. "I'm—I'm glad, Jess. This will mean so much to my grandfather."

Jess shrugged. "Heck, it's the way it should be. There's no finer instrument than a Castille guitar. I wouldn't lend my name to promoting them if I didn't think so. It's a shame the way the company has hung back and somehow gotten itself shuffled off in the depths. You can search long and hard to find a Castille owner and you might as well request the gift of a right arm if you try to borrow it off him. Now maybe we can put a few more of those fine instruments into circulation.''

"Yes." She looked at him gratefully. No matter what her personal feelings were, this was a moment to be treasured. She wanted to remember everything that was said so she could tell her grandfather. He wouldn't give her a moment's peace until she had related every small detail.

"That was one thing I wanted to talk with you about," Jess said. "Then, the other is to invite you to go with us tonight. We're playing a benefit for a music department scholarship fund at U.T.''

"University of Tennessee?"

"Yes. At Knoxville. It's only about three and a half hours from here. We'll drive there in a custom go-cart that isn't exactly the average RV on a dealer's lot.''

So much was happening, Andrea's mind was in a spin trying to deal with all the conflicting emotions warring inside her. Being around Jess was sheer agony. How could she put herself through the kind of evening he suggested? But on the other hand, how could she not? All the work of months was teetering on the brink of success. Would Jess be petty enough to change his mind about the contracts if she refused his invitation? Surely not. But could she dare take the chance?

It wasn't as if she would have to be alone with him. They would be traveling with his entire group. That would give her some insulation from the raw pain of being in his company.

And there was the other matter. She hadn't mentioned it before, but now she knew she must bring it up.

"I have a gift for you," she began, "from my grandfather. I brought it along from Tampa. It's . . . the case is hand-tooled leather, part of my luggage at the hotel. It's a Castille guitar. Your name . . . in pearl insets on the neck."

He gazed at her for a long moment of silence. "A guitar made for me?"

She fought hard not to cringe at the thought of country-western music being played on one of her family's classical instruments.

She was like her grandfather, thinking exactly the way he did about the Castille tradition. Well, she knew she must thicken her skin. The brawl of the marketplace didn't give an E string for tradition. If survival meant a lot of incessant caterwauling with Castilles twanging backup on jukeboxes and low-wattage radio stations from Bangor to San Diego, so be it. At least the instrument would survive and some would find their way into the hands of young graduates from Juilliard.

Jess's eyes were filled with emotion. "I'll treat the guitar as a rare treasure," he said soberly. "It won't find my hands irreverent."

"My grandfather intended for me to present the guitar when you signed the contracts. A bit of an old-world romantic, I suppose. He envisioned a sort of ceremony in what I'm sure you only think of as another piece of business."

"Well," he observed, "it's too bad we won't be able to manage trumpet fanfares and a courtly processional in Randy's office. Sorry about omitting the kind of ritual you'd like."

"I?" She pointed a finger at herself. "Did I say I

Having glimpsed this mad whirligig called Nashville, I'm perfectly willing to accept your signature on the run. I was relaying one of my grandfather's fancies, not my own. And what I was about to say was . . . well, since the contract execution will be but a routine matter fit into the busy schedule of you and your lawyers, why not let me present the guitar now?''

"You mean for me to take along to the U.T. concert? Play it there tonight?"

"Why not?"

"Why not, indeed," he said with a bow of his head. "I would consider it a privilege and an honor. And it would be fitting to have the granddaughter of its maker present when I perform with it in public for the first time."

"Then it's settled. What shall I wear to the concert?"

He shrugged. "Come as you are." He glanced at his watch. "Now that we have that out of the way, I'm afraid we're going to have to drink and run. I'm sure my backup people are wrapping up their bits in retakes, leaving the audio boys to dub and mix. We'll be loading up into the bus in the service area right here behind the building. I'll take you over to your hotel."

"That won't be necessary. You're going to have your hands full seeing the band is settled into the bus. Why don't I just grab a taxi, dash back to the hotel and get the guitar. That will make it simpler for everyone."

She was filled with misgivings as she started back to the hotel. She would feel a lot safer when tonight was behind her and she was safely aboard a flight back to Tampa with the signed contracts.

Chapter Twelve

The "custom go-cart" Jess had talked about turned out to be the largest silver-aluminum bus Andrea had ever seen.

She had barely gotten back to her hotel room when the desk buzzed and told her there was a man downstairs who had been sent by the Jess Clark organization to help her with her things. She'd told the desk clerk to send him up. By the time she was ready to go the tall youth dispatched by Jess had knocked on her door.

She had taken the handsomely tooled leather guitar case from the closet, laid it on the bed, flipped it over and given the beautiful instrument a last-second inspection. The sheen of rich-grained wood had an almost luminescent quality.

Then she'd closed the case and surrendered it to the youth. Picking up her shoulder bag, she'd given the room a final glance and followed the young man downstairs to a waiting taxi. She thought she could have managed perfectly all right by herself. This gesture of sending someone to help her was characteristic of Jess Clark's exaggerated and old-fashioned idea of gallantry toward the "female species."

When they stopped at the parking lot behind the recording studio building, she spotted the bus immediately. There was no way to miss it. It dominated the parking area.

There was a bustle of activity around the custom vehicle. The luggage compartment hatches had been raised to receive the accoutrements of a road trip. Handlers were loading cases containing instruments and a variety of electronic gear comprised of big loudspeakers, control console, microphones, cables. Each piece was carefully arranged to be protected from road hazards such as unexpected shocks and fast stops.

Skeeter was there fussing about his electric bass case. He was carrying his saxophone case under his arm. Peewee and Hooter were having a last stretch before boarding.

Andrea heard Marilee's bright "Hi!" She turned and the fiddle player hurried up to her side and gave her a hug. "Hey, this is a bit of okay! Glad to have you aboard, Andrea."

Marilee's camaraderie was infectious. "I feel like a lucky hitchhiker," Andrea said, laughing.

Then her breath caught in her throat as Jess put in an appearance, stepped down through the open doorway from the interior of the huge bus.

"I'll take these," he said, reaching for the case the

youth was setting down beside Andrea. "Thanks, Tommy."

"Sure thing, Mr. Clark. Anytime."

Jess shook his head at one of the loaders who came around to take the guitar case. "This goes up top. Tender loving care for this baby. It's a Castille straight from the hand of the master maker."

Marilee's eyes widened. "No kidding, Jess?" She looked at Andrea. "You brought it?"

Andrea nodded. "Yes. It's a gift from my grandfather."

"Imagine, a custom-made Castille! Jess, I want to hear you play it tonight."

"You will," Jess promised. "Is there plenty in the galley?"

"As always. Including an extra supply for Skeeter. But I'd better check the ice. Andrea, I'll see you on board." She hopped lightly into the huge vehicle.

Jess said, "Andrea, meet the galoots responsible for our safety and our sound equipment when we get there. Russ Boyd, driver, bodyguard and generally ornery cuss."

"Hello, Russ." Andrea murmured, a bit overwhelmed by the giant towering over her. He was big all over, big head, big shoulders, large feet, huge, scarred hands. His complexion was swarthy. He had a cauliflower ear and a flattened nose, souveniers, Andrea thought, either of the prizefighting ring or barroom brawls. He was dressed in gray twill that showed the darkening of perspiration stains.

"Evenin', ma'am," he said politely with a voice like the low note on a tuba. His homely face split into a disarming grin like that of a friendly St. Bernard. He shook Andrea's hand gently. She smiled, thinking she'd much rather have him for a friend than an enemy.

"And this is Ashley Davidson," Jess added, "otherwise known as 'the Decibel.' He's our property man, the only sound technician working out of Nashville who can take the whisper of silk and turn it into a lion's roar."

"Other way around, you mean, don't you?" Ashley corrected. He was a thin, nervous man well along in years. Lanky, sparse gray hair barely covered his shiny pate. His face was a darker gray, creased and solemn. His voice fitted his looks, a gray and morose echo from his chest. But his eyes still sparkled.

He took Andrea's hand in both of his and gave her a fatherly pat. "Miss Castille, I got a spare pair of earplugs in case you need them."

"Listen to that!" Jess chided with a grin. "Decibel, the closest you'll ever get to heaven is Jess Clark singing like a cherub."

The sound man gave Andrea a secret wink and twirled a forefinger close to his temple. "Horse kicked him in the head once," he confided.

Andrea felt her spirits rising and flowing out to these people. One second a stranger, the next pal, friend, companion as far as Russ and Ashley were concerned. It was perhaps another tiny insight. In an existence of shifting sand, transitory careers with frightful casualty rates, why bother with reserve? There was neither time nor circumstances for the formal approach.

"I know," Andrea said, responding to Ashley's teasing mood. "Poor horse!"

"I think," Jess said to no one in particular, "I smell a gang-up. Come on, beautiful, into the bus with you!"

They climbed aboard. Andrea heard the thud and click of metal as the luggage compartment was closed and locked.

Her immediate impression was one of a plush playroom. The seats and couches were covered in crushed velour that looked downy soft. The gallery area was an ultracompact arrangement of stovetop, sink, refrigerator, bar, storage cabinets and a small microwave. Wedged next to the galley was a panel of a doorway that Andrea guessed was a compact restroom. Midway between the galley and front, a thirteen-inch color television set with VCR tape deck attached, anchored like everything else, awaited the flicking of a switch. There were even storage cabinets and a small closet arranged between seats and couches. It was, indeed, a fully equipped, luxurious abode on wheels.

Andrea realized she was standing on the entryway step, simply staring and blocking the doorway. Lowering her head slightly, she moved on up and slipped into the empty seat beside Marilee in response to Marilee's smiling invitation.

Still looking around at the sheen of chrome, wood paneling and plush upholstery, Andrea murmured, "I have only one word for it: Wow!"

"Wait'll you feel the ride," Marilee said. "It's like floating on a feather. Sure beats the heck out of the old days when you jumped five hundred miles through sleet, fog or rain between one-nighters, your worldly goods under a tarp on a battered old pickup truck, your fingers crossed to keep the clattering engine from throwing a rod before you pulled into the next honky-tonk."

Russ had settled in the driver's seat, Jess standing

braced beside him and saying something about I-240 repairs detouring traffic on the Knoxville approach.

Russ touched a lever and the door closed. Then, with a turn of the ignition key, the powerful diesel rumbled into life. Russ slowly turned left, and they were off.

Still thinking of Marilee's words and the harsh realities they had expressed, Andrea said, "I guess musicians never forget the early, hard times."

"Can't afford to, Andrea. When you're out there tuckered, but you've got to come up with one more big smile, one more little lively bow, one more big sockeroo note, you gulp. Surprising how it can jolt you into reaching way down inside for that extra measure of performance. I think it's called running scared."

"Ever think of quitting?"

Marilee looked at Andrea as if not entirely comprehending the question. "Why on earth would I ever want to do that? It's our life. Might take a break sometime to have a youngster or two. But quit? Girl, whatever would I do? This is my life."

Jess had moved back to the galley. Hooter was stretched on a sofalike seat with obvious intent to nap. Skeeter was hunched at the TV set, fiddling with power and antenna directional controls. Peewee had temporarily disappeared into the mini–comfort station. Ashley the Decibel was hunched in a forward seat watching the scenery as the urban setting began to dissolve into rural countryside. Behind them were the two husky young handlers who would unpack and set up the equipment when they arrived at the concert site.

"Taking orders for supper!" Jess called out.

Hooter sat up. "What's on the menu?"

"I gotta lotsa microwavey really good stuff!" Jess parodied. "I gotta hotsa pastrami on rye. I gotta shrimper, she'sa Creole. I gotta da hamburger. I gotta fried chicken your mama she'sa tried to make. I gotta—"

"Any of those hotdogs with mustard, onions and chili?" Skeeter asked.

"Boy, I gotta so many dogs she'sa coon-hunt pack. You wanna how many?"

"Four," Skeeter said, "and a bottle of beer."

"Whassa mat? You a growin' boy. You need your nourishment. You off-a you appetite or somethin'?"

Jess scrubbed his hands at the sink preparatory to flicking latches and switches, setting out prepackaged food for the microwave, plastic plates and cutlery.

Thus began the miles of pleasantly rolling countryside. The palatial van somehow had a magic-carpet effect, a miniworld of elegance and comfort.

While everyone was busy eating, Marilee engaged in woman-to-woman gossip about the background of the musicians in Jess's group. "Peewee comes from Alabama pecan people and Skeeter's family are well-to-do names in the Nashville social register. Hooter . . . well, I guess you could describe his family as frayed blue collar. My family was upper middle class. Jess, now, is something else. At least we had homes. We never had to grapple a rocky coal-country mountainside field hoping to find one more turnip. How he clawed his way out of those coal mines and hobo jungles to get on top without it making him the most arrogant, conceited guy in town I'll never know."

Skeeter, having wolfed down the four hotdogs and

pitcher of beer, fooled with the TV set some more; then, not finding a program that satisfied him, he turned it off. With nothing better to do, he decided to entertain himself. A few mellow notes came from his direction.

Looking over her shoulder, Andrea saw him slouched on the edge of a seat resting the sax on his knee while he made an adjustment to the reed. Then he blew a fast arpeggio, a swift passage that smacked of Boots Randolph. Then he was off on a wild, carefree rendition of a piece that was reminiscent of an energetic barn dance: couples twirling, swirling, their feet clogging a machine-gun tempo.

Before Skeeter was halfway through the chorus, Hooter, roused from his nap, had slipped a pair of wire drum brushes from a pocket and was laying down a beat on a practice pad.

Andrea sensed the spontaneous response in Marilee who had been clicking her fingers from the very first measure.

"Now ain't that kid something?" she asked with an impulsive outburst of enthusiasm.

Although the melody was strange and Skeeter's improvisations were new to Andrea's musical experience, she instantly recognized that Marilee had stated only part of it. Skeeter was very something, and Hooter was thumping a beat with snap-brush counterpoint. Two men in communion, sensing instinctively the other's ideas.

"Lord!" Marilee complained. "You'd think we'd get enough of it working for a paycheck. . . ."

But this wasn't paycheck stuff and Marilee was laughing tolerantly at herself as she was out of her seat and scrambling for a fiddle stashed in one of the overhead cabinets. In less than a minute a double-bowed countermelody was underscoring Skeeter's intricacies.

Peewee had been content to lounge on a seat, absorbed in a magazine. Now he pitched the periodical aside and flipped open the piano keyboard of a mini, portable synthesizer.

He caught Skeeter at the beginning of an eight-bar phrase and his unlikely fingers played a chord that was as crystalline as a waterfall in high-mountain country. Skeeter's sax searched for the note that would never be there. But he found it on a chorus and immediately the horn peeled away like a high-flying plane in a wingover and laid a sustained pattern of sound for the fiddle to rise to new heights. And after Marilee's search and discovery of sounds sensed in a woodlands on a dewy morning, it was Peewee's turn. He teased with a tentative single note. Then an afterbeat answered and soon all the voices under his fingertips were rising in a hallelujah chorus.

All of it was joined and unified by the sheer energy of Hooter's cohesive beat.

It seemed to Andrea that the bus itself had drawn carefree animation from the unshackled expressions. Ashley was clicking his fingers, his morose face lighted by a huge grin. The young luggage handlers were patting their feet. Andrea couldn't keep her own feet still. Russ was keeping time on the steering wheel rim and in a gravelly, absolutely tone-deaf voice was softly venting the lyrics to himself, a folkish little story that Andrea caught from the bus driver in snatches. It related the situation of a po'-devil logger who'd spent a week in Smoky Mountain timber country manhandling a big chain saw, sledgehammers and wedges, snaking the giant trees out. Saturday night in town he'd blown his paycheck shindigging and boozing and on Sunday morning, while proper folks were in church, the horribly hungover po' devil was out trying to find somebody with at least a slug of home brew because his gal had poured out the remaining hair of the dog he'd staggered home with last night.

They built a final chorus as an entity, and in the sudden silence Russ beeped a two-note tag from the bus horn.

The style wasn't familiar, but Andrea knew musicians' music when she heard it and she was well aware that she had been treated to the twenty-four-carat article.

"I believe that grabbed you a little," Jess said, taking a seat beside Andrea.

"Who could resist such . . ." Andrea became acutely conscious of Jess sitting close to her. She drew a cooling breath. "Where did it come from? Who wrote it?"

"Who knows?" Jess said. "It was one of those songs that just somehow write themselves. The words change with the setting and with the times. In one section of Appalachia, po' devil would be a miner instead of a logger. The song in west Texas makes him a cowpuncher. A generation ago, the logger would have been using double-bitted axes instead of chain saws. These days, the words might change to make him the driver of an eighteen-wheeler. Just one of those things out of a misty past. Somebody sings it on the porch of somebody's cabin and that somebody embellishes it a little and sings it at a Saturday-night dance. I suppose it finally got written down somewhere."

"What's the matter with you, Jess?" the Decibel called from the front. "Cat got your fingers?"

A chorus of recriminations were heaped on Jess for not having joined the jam session in his usual way.

He smiled softly. "A fellow likes to be begged a little," which got him a response of affable catcalls and jeers.

Andrea watched him lift the Castille and rest it on a countertop, carefully opening the case. He studied the instrument, turning it lovingly in his hands, his eyes not missing a detail. It was the most beautiful of guitars, its finish like satin, his name in soft pearl along the neck, the frets fitted in tolerances calipered in ten-thousandths for perfect intonation.

Sitting on the edge of a couch, he rested the guitar on his knee and turned it expertly. Andrea's own natural musical ear was excellent. She suspected that Jess was one of those rare people born with perfect pitch, who could name the key that had been struck on a piano across the street or the exact frequency on the musical scale of a train whistle on a lonely night.

He strummed a broad, basic major chord and the Castille responded with the subdued majesty of an organ murmuring in a nave. Jess's eyes lighted with admiration and delight.

He paused and was thoughtful for a moment. "I wish the instrument's maker could have been here. Even so, the first one is for him, your grandfather, Andrea. I hope it will express something of my appreciation."

And with that he struck a broad augmented chord while the little finger of his left hand grumbled a chromatic bass. A second chord followed. The bass became a recalcitrant rebel.

Andrea stared at him. This was no country-western

picking. Was he actually capable of playing the kind of music her grandfather would most enjoy hearing on the guitar?

She couldn't believe what her ears were hearing. She sat now with bated breath. He was actually into it, the famous Malagueña by Ernesto Lecuona. One of the most challenging solos by a modern composer, Malagueña wasn't frequently included as a repertory number for performance by guitarists because of its demands on the performer. It was Flamenco guitar but the kind of flamenco heard in concert halls.

Here again was more musician's music. This time, wonder of wonders, on a classical level!

Andrea sat entranced, unable to move, letting the stirring beauty of the music pour through her.

Images of Spain were awakened in Andrea's mind by the music. She wasn't sure if her images were the fantasies Lecuona had intended to evoke, nor did she care. If someone else found a different shading of meaning in the music—in any musical composition—they were entitled. It was all subjective anyway.

He was approaching that challenging passage where all ten fingers were like the darting tongues of snakes.

It was the right hand busy with full chord melody, the thumb dropping bass notes like the thunder of a flamenco dancer's heels, the left hand single-stringing a fiery counter-melody.

Andrea fell back, letting out a breath. She'd heard her grandfather do Malagueña, but never quite like this, leaving a spellbinding silence in its wake. Only Montoya could have put Jess Clark in the shade tonight.

She was speechless, stunned with unbelieving surprise. Never in her wildest dreams had she imagined Jess was capable of that kind of virtuosity or had ever even heard of Lecuona's composition. By what miracle, where in the hobo camps, in the boxcars, in the smoky honky-tonks and sleazy motels, had he learned of Malagueña? And— greater miracle—how had he developed the skill to play it? Another paradox, another unsolved mystery of the man, Jess Clark.

Then, without fanfare, the richness of his voice and that of the guitar blended into an old hymn about a little church in the wildwood. Then, a quick one-stroke modulation and he was into the story of a coal miner coughing out his lungs in the dark depths, down in the bowls of the earth. Next, the song about a harried sheriff in high-speed pursuit around mountainous hairpin curves, trying to catch the bootlegger who was the bane of his existence. And for added measure there was a change of tempo and the doleful complaint of a fellow who loved his pickup truck because she was the only female critter who had never done him wrong.

The last note died away. Again the hushed silence. Only the sibilant, ghostly singing of the wheels on the pavement below. Jess said quietly, "Andrea, tell your grandfather for me that it's quite an instrument."

She nodded, not trusting herself to speak. She felt as if she'd been caught short by a glimpse at things she'd always suspected were there but which she'd never really been able to grasp. She was beginning to understand how Jess had chosen his métier. No, she corrected that. He'd not had a choice in the matter. He had been destined from the beginning for this—this genius. She had no other word for it. His life was the music that expressed the earthy human story of a childhood of grinding poverty, a father dying like the one in the song, the bitter struggle out of the pit to where he was now. It was music expressive of a soul. And in the soul of Jess Clark was an expression of all who'd struggled, from the first pioneer building a log cabin to the slum-dwelling kid of today with a head full of dreams.

"I will tell my grandfather," Andrea said quietly, "that the guitar is in the best of hands."

Chapter Thirteen

*T*he Knoxville skyline was getting closer. They swooped down a freeway ramp, into the jam and noise of city traffic, past buildings and locations that had been revamped by the World's Fair that had taken place in Knoxville a couple of years previously.

Then they were into the relative serenity of the sprawling campus of one of the larger state universities. Darkness had fallen. Andrea glimpsed the old vine-covered brick wall of a large building in the sweep of headlights as Russ braked the bus to an easy stop.

There were rising, stretching figures about her now, and Andrea could sense the preperformance tension. Outside were shadowy figures in the glow of street lamps. College students were beginning to drift toward the bus, whistling and yelling greetings. Jess bent at a window to smile and wave. He turned to the others in the bus. "We're beginning to cut our setup time pretty short. Better get a move on."

Marilee slipped her arm through Andrea's as they began moving toward the open door of the bus. "The good ones are always so uptight they feel sure they'll blow a gasket this time," she said. "But somehow when that curtain goes up, it takes the preconcert jittery feeling right with it. Then the adrenaline starts flowing and you wouldn't be anyplace else in the world for a million bucks."

There followed total confusion. Jess was almost mobbed as he emerged from the bus. Ashley the Decibel was already outside, opening the luggage compartment and overseeing the unloading and transport of equipment to the stage inside. He snapped orders to the two husky handlers and to some strapping youths in the excited crowd who offered assistance.

Andrea felt a moment of panic in the crush of bodies around them. She was grateful for the reassuring touch of Marilee's hand on her arm. "Just stick close," Marilee said in her ear. "The stage door is only a few feet away and Russ knows his job."

While Jess bantered and touched reaching hands, Russ had them in swift motion as a group. In moments they were inside, door closing on the fans.

They walked down a dim corridor where naked bulbs shed light through wire cages. Andrea accompanied Marilee into a dressing room. The costume cases arrived shortly. Marilee changed into her performing outfit, a saucy, above-the-knee cowgirl skirt, flaming-red blouse of silk and sequins, calf-high western boots and fringed vest. Her western hat had a cord under her chin so the hat could be shoved back off her lovely head to dangle between her shoulders during the performance.

Marilee opened her makeup kit, looked at her reflected image in a large mirror encircled with light bulbs. She sat briefly at the dressing table to give herself final touches with brush, fingertips and powder puff.

"Look okay?" she asked, rising to face Andrea.

"Like a doll under the tree on Christmas morning," Andrea said truthfully.

Marilee laughed, wrinkling her nose. "Well, it'll have to do. I'll never have what you were born with, Andrea. Danged freckles! Anyway, come on. Let's move. Still have to get tuned and ready."

Andrea was escorted to a spot in the wings to watch the performance. From the babble out beyond the closed curtain she was sure there was a standing-room-only crowd.

Somehow, order emerged from chaos and they were all in place on the stage, holding instruments at the ready, the men in their eye-catching western garb, eyes on Jess's upraised hand. His other hand was resting lightly on the neck of the Castille, which he wore in standing position with a shoulder strap of heavy silver, gold-and-black brocade with tassels at the ends that secured it to the guitar.

His hand came down and the music exploded as the curtain began to rise, revealing the Jess Clark group in the silver magic of stage lights. From the packed house came a thunderous roar.

The intro was fast and short, giving the audience the chance to vent their enthusiastic welcome and settle down. Jess stood at the mike, looking out over the sea of faces.

His timing was superb, Andrea thought. He let just the right fraction of silence elapse. Then, as if those dark, expressive eyes were singling out everyone before him individually, his tone instantly made him an old friend. "Hello, you cotton-pickin' Volunteers!"

The walls shook from the response.

He talked to them in his infectious, lazy stage drawl, and he had them in his power from that moment, bringing laughter, the catch of a sob, peaks of excitement and hushed moments when not a muscle moved in all the vast audience.

Andrea fell under a spell all her own, the personal pain she felt becoming all the more acute because of the Jess Clark charm that radiated like waves of irresistible magnetism. *Damn you, Jess Clark,* she thought, fighting back tears. *Why did I have to go and fall in love with you? I'm going to go back home tomorrow and I'll never completely get over you.*

She lost sense of time and place, overpowered by the dazzling showmanship, the earthen energy of the music. It was an experience of raw emotion, with moments of excitement that made the heart race, then a change of tempo to a reflective, sentimental mood that would bring a tear.

At one point, she realized with a shock that the performance was eliciting from her the same response as from the audience. Had Jess converted her to liking his kind of music? She didn't know how she would feel about it tomorrow, but for this evening he had surely made a hand-clapping, foot-stomping country-western fan out of her.

When it was over, her emotions felt as if they reluctantly had to come back to reality.

They lined up out on the stage for a final bow before the multitude that was on its collective feet, applauding, whistling, stamping, yelling his name.

The curtain swept down and the house lights went up. While the crowd began milling, talking, moving toward the exits, Jess and his people walked tiredly into the wing where Andrea stood.

Jess was soaked with perspiration, droplets still standing on his forehead. His eyes had a glazed, drained look. He paused before Andrea, wiping his face with a handkerchief. His mouth was curved in a lopsided grin. "Want my autograph, lady?"

She tried to pull her gaze from him, to deaden the wrenching pain. "It—it was an exciting performance, Jess," she somehow managed to say.

"Thank you," he replied humbly. "We try to do our best. Now I've got to get cleaned up. See you on the bus."

The return trip to Nashville was subdued. There was no jam session. Very little talk. Just tired people sinking into the comfort of the bus, indistinct in the near darkness of its haven. Lights were out. Up ahead at the steering wheel, Russ was a blocky, comforting silhouette in the flashing headlight glow of approaching cars. Below them all, the huge tires whispered a soft, soothing lullaby in the dead hours when most of the world had gone to sleep.

They had stopped briefly at a late-night drive-through

snack bar west of Knoxville. Then the bus had mounted the interstate for the unbroken run home.

When they had entered the bus after the concert, Andrea had headed again for a place beside Marilee. To her consternation, Jess had captured her arm in a firm grip and directed her to a seat with him at the rear of the bus.

Andrea watched the pale moonlight on distant fields they passed. She thought of how much Jess had given of himself tonight. Even though he had changed clothes before leaving the auditorium, he still felt damp with fatigue. Much to her relief, he had little to say. She hoped he would doze off, as had the others, making the trip back less painful for her. She had nothing more to say to him now. All she wanted was to escape to the safety of her hotel room and the final countdown to the time the contracts were signed and she was on the plane home.

But in the darkness, he reached for her hand. She stiffened, her breath catching in her throat. He put a finger against her chin, turning her face gently toward his. He was going to kiss her. Panic erupted in her. She turned away.

There was a moment of painful, heavy silence. Jess asked softly, "What is it, Andrea?"

Her mouth was dry. She was at a loss to know how to answer him.

"Have I done something to make you angry?"

Her thoughts were flying off in all directions. She wondered desperately how to handle this situation. She had thought it would be safe to accept the invitation to go with the group to the concert. They would be in a crowded bus. At no time would she have to be alone with Jess.

She hadn't counted on the size of this giant vehicle, which had successfully isolated them in this dark, rear seat. She hadn't anticipated everyone else going to sleep.

More than anything she had wanted to avoid a confrontation with Jess until after the contracts were signed and tucked safely into her briefcase. Then, if necessary, she could tell him off. But not now. Not when an eruption of bitter words might kill the chance to save Castille Guitars at the last minute.

She could force herself to be cordial to him, somehow manage to smile and act pleasant and hide the fact that she hated him. But there was a certain point beyond which she could not be a hypocrite. There was no way she could force herself to endure his kiss.

She couldn't think what to say, so she said nothing.

But he wasn't about to let the matter drop. "I thought we had something great going for us," Jess went on. "Then, you suddenly turned cold as a Russian winter."

"Let's just say I had second thoughts and let it go at that. . . ."

"No, I'm not going to let it go at that!" he said in a low, angry tone. "You owe me an explanation, Andrea."

"Jess, everybody is tired. Let's wait until tomorrow."

She could feel his angry gaze slashing into her in the darkness. "No, we're going to settle this right now."

He was pushing her to the ragged edge. She tried to stifle the words, but they wrenched their way from between her stiff lips. "Jess, you're not being fair to me. Especially, you're not being fair to Nori."

There was a moment of silence. His gaze intensified, making her feel impaled. "What has Nori got to do with this?" he asked huskily.

"You know."

"No. Would you care to explain?"

Tearfully, she said, "Jess, please, couldn't we just drop the matter?"

"After what you just said? You'd better make yourself a little clearer, Andrea."

She closed her eyes against the tears that seeped from under her long lashes. "Jess, Nori told me how things are between the two of you. Last night at Skyland, I helped her get into bed. When I put her things in the closet, I saw that she has been living with you."

Jess slowly let his breath out. "Now I understand why you suddenly got a headache last night! Andrea, Nori has been living at Skyland for a couple of weeks. She has not been living with me. There's a difference. She hit rock bottom. Things got so bad for her, she was kicked out of her apartment because she's two months behind on her rent. We've all been trying to save her from going completely over the edge. This recording deal today was her big chance. I wanted to get her out of the city, away from the temptation of bars and that crowd of so-called friends that follows her around. I offered her Skyland for a couple of weeks if she'd promise to stay dry. She was doing pretty good until yesterday, when I guess she got a bad case of stage fright. The point is, I don't spend all my time at Skyland. I have too many things to take care of in town, so I keep an apartment there and that's where I've been for most of the time the past couple of weeks."

Andrea sat still as the words slowly sank in. A glimmer of joy began to tentatively come alive, like morning rays of sunrise splitting a black night's horizon. Dare she believe he was telling the truth? Caution told her to be skeptical. He would naturally lie, wouldn't he? But she wanted so much to believe him!

"Nori said—"

"Don't pay any attention to Nori, Andrea," he interrupted impatiently. "You know she'd been drinking. When she's like that she's liable to say anything."

"I—I want to believe you, Jess."

"Then do."

His voice was low so the others sitting up front wouldn't hear, but it was strong and convincing. The strength of his hand holding her fingers urged her to believe him. The spell he had cast over her along with his audience tonight still had her in its grip. He was the most dynamic man she had ever known. Right now, she could feel the magnetism of his personality enveloping her, sapping her resistance, turning caution to mush. . . .

"Jess . . ." Her voice trembled.

Again he turned her face to his. This time she lacked the strength to resist. His lips were on hers, moist, tender, gentle in their demand. Her response overwhelmed her. Their bodies moved closer. The circle of his embrace was a quiet warmth tempered by the outpouring of all his vital energies out there on the stage tonight.

He made the bus seem like the warm, protective shelter of a cave. As if wishing to memorize every line and hollow, his free hand softly traced the curves of her body, thigh, hips, waist, teasing lingeringly across the swell of her breast. A liquid feeling of comfort and delight stole through her.

The joy that suffused her being had dispelled the darkness completely. There was a singing inside letting her love for Jess flow freely again.

She felt like laughing aloud for joy. Her anger and disillusionment had just been a ridiculous mistake, a comedy of errors! In a blinding moment, all of her tender feeling for him returned. Excitement bubbled through her veins.

She nestled closer in the warmth of his arms against the stalwart bulk of his chest. Her head rested on his shoulder, her parted lips breathing softly against the column of his neck.

She was drifting on a pleasant sea . . . the two of them drifting away in each other's arms. . . .

Her next awareness came from a gentle touch on her shoulder, the soft pronouncement of her name. "Andrea. We're here—back home."

She opened her eyes, needing a moment to orient herself. She realized she'd drifted off to sleep in Jess's embrace. Jess, too, was asleep.

Now she could see Russ's smiling face hovering over the seat. "Hi, kid," Russ whispered. Except for the guarded sound of his voice, the bus was heavy with silence. Everyone was sleeping. They were insulated from the sounds of early traffic trickling past in the first gray light of dawn.

She raised her head and saw that Russ had stopped the bus before the entrance to her hotel. She nodded and eased apart from Jess, careful not to awaken him. He stirred, shifted his position slightly and went on sleeping.

Slipping from the seat, she paused to smile at the peaceful expression on his sleeping face. Relaxed and wholly unguarded, with a lock of hair tumbled carelessly over his forehead, his face reflected a boyishness. The long black lashes made her want to lean forward and give the closed eyelids a tender kiss.

Instead, she eased farther forward. Careful not to disturb anyone, Russ followed her to the front door of the bus. "Would you like some help, Andrea?"

"Of course not! All I have to carry is my small case. Russ, thanks for everything."

In her room, she changed into pale-blue pajamas and stretched against the luxury of the bed. She lay pensively, staring at the dark ceiling, trying to grasp all that had happened in the past twenty-four hours. It was almost more than her emotional capabilities could absorb. Already the long, long day and night were taking on the unreal aspects of a dream. Had she really ridden the bus to Knoxville? Had that inspired concert been for real? Had Jess held her in his arms, reassuring her that she had been mistaken about his involvement with Nori? Had it all been real or a fantasy?

She tried to grapple with the impact of what all this meant to her life, but it dissolved into that shadowy world between sleep and dreams and then faded away completely. . . .

She awoke with a start. She'd been dreaming of a bus floating in space between the stars.

Then she heard again what had awakened her, a tapping at her door. She flung back the sheet, glancing at her watch. Good grief! It was high noon.

This time the rapping of knuckles was louder. "Be right with you!" Andrea called as she looked for a light robe to fling over her pajamas.

Finally, she opened the door and felt as if she'd been

slapped. Nori Lawrence was the last person she'd expected to see.

The petite blonde was a distinct contrast to the way she had looked on their two previous meetings. Today Nori looked younger, freshly innocent. The marvelous turn her life had taken had apparently worked a near miracle. Andrea realized with a small shock that this was the first time she had seen Nori cold sober.

"Sorry to break in and wake you, Andrea, but I had to catch you on the run. Thank heaven, it's going to be like the old days again, never a minute to catch my breath!" She laughed, a self-effacing note. "Of course I have to thank Jess for that. Didn't do it all myself, did I? And this time it's going to be different. No better way to learn a lesson than the hard way, the way I learned, I guess. This go-round there'll be a steady stream of Nori Lawrence albums stacked in all the music stores."

"Come in, Nori."

"Just for a minute. I ducked by to give you this. Jess sent it over." She held out a thick manila envelope. "It's the contracts, all checked over and okayed by Jess's lawyers. He's been over there since ten o'clock. Signed, sealed and now delivered—the thing you came to Nashville for. I guess you and I both have something to celebrate. Your grandfather will be proud of you."

Somewhat dazed, Andrea took the package. Welling up in her was a tremendous sense of relief. It was over, the weeks of tension, the disappointing delays, the strain she had been under since she came to Nashville. Here, in her hands, she held the future of Castille Guitars—a happy, prosperous future.

But then her personal involvement surfaced. "Did—did Jess send any kind of message?"

Nori shook her head. "Nope. He's pretty busy today. Just wanted to make sure you got the contracts by noon. Guess you have an early flight to catch back to Tampa."

Nori's eyes lighted up. "Speaking of Jess, look what he surprised me with this morning." She dangled a left hand in front of Andrea's eyes. The diamond on her ring finger was blinding.

Time seemed to stop. Faintly, Andrea was aware of the distant, muffled sound of traffic in the street below. There was the rumble of the elevator door out in the hall. An air-conditioner duct whispered softly.

She saw her reflection in the dresser mirror. All the blood had drained from her face. Her voice seemed to echo from a distant chasm. "It's a lovely ring, Nori. . . ."

"Yeah, when Jess does something, he does it right. He promised an engagement ring if I pulled myself together and did the recording. Looks like he's going to make an honest woman out of me at last. Hope you can fly back for the wedding."

"Wedding?" Andrea whispered.

"Yep. He's set the date and everything."

"I—I didn't know. . . ."

Nori raised an eyebrow, giving her a quizzical, searching look. "Jess didn't tell you how things are between him and me? No, I guess he wouldn't. Hope you didn't let yourself take his little fling with you too seriously. A girl could get hurt real bad, messing with Jess Clark. I could tell when I saw you out at the Quackendalls' cookout that

Jess had his sights leveled on you for a conquest. When he goes after something, he generally gets it, one way or the other. He never would have gotten where he is today if he didn't have that ruthless streak. I figure that you were a real challenge to him, something different from the kind of corn-fed bar hoppers he's used to—a real cool, aristocratic lady. His ego must have gone into high gear. Jess Clark would do anything, say anything, tell any kind of lie to get something once he's made up his mind he wants it. How else do you think he's made it to the top of the heap? He stepped on a lot of little people getting up there."

Then she shrugged. "Well, that's okay. Jess and I understand each other. We're made up of the same kind of stuff, one-tenth talent and nine-tenths trash. Did you know I grew up in Jess's hometown?"

Andrea tried to swallow. She shook her head, dazed and sick.

"Yeah, I've known Jess all my life. I put up with a lot from that bastard. But"—she shrugged—"he always comes back to me. And that's worth something."

She chewed her lip thoughtfully. "Oh, by the way, this ought to give your guitar promotion a real big boost. Jess has been picked to receive the top country-western singer of the year award. He just got word this morning. There's going to be a big bash at the Kennedy Center in Washington, D.C., honoring him ten days from now. I reckon everybody includin' the president and first lady will be there. It'll be on national TV. Isn't that something? Back home, nobody thought Jess would amount to a hill of beans." She laughed. "Jess said we'll tie the knot right after the awards event. Now won't that be somethin' to look forward to? Well, you got a plane to catch and I've got an appointment to talk business with some recording executives types. Wish me luck.''

She waved and then Andrea was staring at the closed door.

Two hours later, Andrea was in an airliner. The city of Nashville was a toy village thousands of feet below, dissolving in the distance. She felt drained and empty. She supposed the tears would come later when the shock wore off and the pain became real.

Chapter Fourteen

*A*ndrea temporarily buried her own heartache under the surface of her triumphant return. Again Raymond met her at the Tampa airport. He swooped her into a bear hug with a display of exuberance uncharacteristic of his usual reserve.

They hurried to the hospital, where Andrea found her grandfather propped up in bed. She placed the signed contracts in his hands. The light that sprang alive in his eyes was a balm to the aching hurt inside her. Years melted from the lined face. The worry that had haunted his expression for so many weeks disappeared.

"This is going to make the difference, isn't it, Raymond?" he asked, anxiously waving the contracts. "The advertising promotion you've talked about . . . you can proceed now, can't you?"

"Absolutely," Raymond replied. "The plans are all

laid out by the advertising agency that will handle the details. All we've been waiting for is Jess Clark's signature. In a few weeks Castille Guitars will become a household word from coast to coast.''

Manola Castille slapped his fist into his palm. ''We've done it! Excellent!'' He gazed at Andrea with tears in his eyes. ''My granddaughter, my child. How can I thank you for what you have accomplished? These papers you brought back from Nashville may be our salvation.''

''Abuelo, I did nothing except take them to Nashville. I was nothing more than a delivery person. The credit goes to you and Raymond for the long negotiations that led up to this point.''

''Then the credit goes to all of us. Just wait until I get out of this place! We'll have such a celebration as you wouldn't believe. A banquet, a fiesta for everyone in the plant.''

''Oh, here's another bit of news that may be important.'' Andrea drew a breath, making a determined effort to keep her personal feelings under control. ''Just before I left Nashville today, I learned that Jess Clark has been picked to receive the award as the top country and western entertainer of the year. There will be a national TV broadcast of the event from Kennedy Center in a week.''

''Marvelous!'' Raymond exclaimed. ''What luck! Our fortunes appear to have taken a positive turn.''

''What does it mean to us?'' Manola asked, looking a fle bewildered.

''Why, it gives additional impact to our advertising campaign!'' Raymond explained. ''Not only do we have a well-known figure in the field of popular music endorsing our product—we'll have the top country-western entertainer of the year!''

''Good, good!'' Manola Castille nodded. ''Why they make such awards and such a fuss over that kind of music is beyond me, but I shouldn't look a gift horse in the mouth, eh?'' He chuckled.

''Abuelo, last night I went to one of Jess Clark's performances,'' Andrea said quietly. ''Before I heard him perform in person I was like you. I had little use for his kind of music. But I have to give him credit. Whatever personal shortcomings he has, his talent before an audience transcends the musical form. I can only describe him as some kind of dynamic genius. And—Abuelo—this you may find hard to believe, but when I presented the special guitar to him, do you know the first thing he played on it? Ernesto Lecuona's Malagueña.''

Manola's eyes widened in surprised disbelief. Malagueña? He could play it?''

''Flawlessly. You would have been gratified to hear such a beautiful rendition from the instrument of your making, Abuelo. And before he played it, he said to tell you that he played it for you.''

Manola shook his head. ''Perhaps I have underestimated the man.''

Andrea felt her strength ebbing. She had made superhuman demands on her will to hide her own despair and keep a cheerful front. Now she was exhausted. She needed desperately to find a quiet place to be alone with her heartache.

''I was up late last night at the Jess Clark concert,'' she said. ''I rode with the group to Knoxville. I'm really worn out. If you don't mind, Raymond, I'd appreciate it if you could take me to my apartment so I can get some rest."

"Yes, of course!" cried her grandfather. "You go rest, child. Sleep around the clock. There'll be plenty of time to talk and celebrate."

She kissed his forehead, then she and Raymond walked to the door. She glanced back once. Manola's eyes were closed; his lips moved silently and he crossed himself. She knew he was saying a prayer of thanksgiving.

"Don't let us down now, Raymond," Andrea said as they drove to her apartment. "We've promised him so much."

Raymond smiled broadly. "I have every confidence in the world in the promotion, Andrea. With Jess Clark's name on those contracts, doors will open for new lines of credit. I can just about guarantee that a year from now Castille Guitars will be a bustling factory with shifts working around the clock."

Andrea sighed. "Then maybe the price wasn't too high to pay. . . ." she murmured to herself.

"What?"

"Nothing. Just thinking aloud."

There was a pause. Then Raymond asked, "Andrea, have you given any more thought to my proposal?"

She bit her lip. "Raymond, the past few days my life has been a whirlpool. Forgive me. I—I just don't have an answer for you now." She gave his hand a squeeze. "Give me time to sort some things out in my mind, okay?"

How would she feel about marrying Raymond a month from now—six months from now? She had no way of knowing. The hurt over Jess Clark was too raw. Maybe in time, when the wound healed a bit, she might reconsider Raymond's proposal. Marrying him would be the sensible, sane thing to do. Everything connected with Jess Clark had been insanity. Thinking back over the events of the past days, she found it hard to believe that she, Andrea Castille, could have behaved in such a rash, impulsive, irrational manner. How could a man turn her well-ordered life totally upside down like that? Was he some kind of Svengali who could mesmerize people? After seeing how he had captured, charmed and entranced an audience, she could half believe it. Under his spell she had lost all perspective, all restraint.

At last they arrived at her apartment. Within the safe seclusion of its walls, she fell into bed, too exhausted to get out of her clothes. She felt utterly drained.

Sometime during the night, the tears came—raw, wracking sobs that shook her entire body. Hurt and anger were there, mingled with a terrible sense of loss. How cruel it had been of him to lie to her on the bus! She was coping with the hurtful truth, that Nori was his mistress and he had cheated on her to have his little fling with Andrea. And then on the bus ride back from Knoxville, with his smooth lies and phony sincerity, he'd had her believing he was being honest with her. What a charade! What a despicable cad he was!

As much as she grieved for her own betrayal, she felt sorry for poor little Nori Lawrence. What humiliation the girl must endure just to doggedly hang on to that man! There had to be an element of masochism involved.

At last, emotionally and physically exhausted, Andrea fell into a deep, sodden sleep.

She felt she'd hardly closed her eyes when she opened

them again. It was midmorning! Her eyes felt puffy, her mind full of cobwebs from the deathlike sleep.

She lay staring at the ceiling enveloped in a cloud of depression. To drag herself out of bed and out of her wrinkled clothes seemed impossible.

Then, dimly through her befuddled senses, she realized she had been awakened by voices out in the hallway. She frowned, gradually becoming more aware, her fogged mind groping toward making identification.

One was the familiar voice of Mr. Garcia, the building super.

The other . . . a familiarity, too, but impossible, of course. A trick of her distraught emotions . . . and yet . . .

She sat up, groggy, confused, trying to separate hallucination from reality.

That voice again, awakening a thousand wrenching emotions. She pressed her palms against her flushed cheeks, fingertips on throbbing temples. *Get hold of yourself, girl! Has this thing pushed you over the edge?*

A knock at her door.

She sat immobilized, eyes wide and stricken, a fixed stare at the door.

The knock again. The voice. "Andrea."

Something like a whimper escaped her pale lips. She shook her head slowly in stunned disbelief.

She drew a ragged breath. If she was hallucinating, this was frighteningly real. And it wouldn't go away.

Somehow she found the strength to go to the door. With icy, trembling fingers, she opened locks, turned the knob.

Jess Clark strode into the room. She heard him mutter, "Had a devil of a time finding you. . . ."

She stood rooted to the floor. Her mouth felt stuffed with cotton. Somehow she got the words out. "What are you doing here?"

"What do you think? Trying to find out what possessed you to pull that disappearing act!"

She felt the powerful grip of his hands on her arms, the impact of his intense, dark-eyed gaze. She hated herself for that uncontrollable wave of yearning that made her heart ache at his touch even now in spite of his duplicity. Was this the kind of weakness that made Nori his willing slave?

"You look awful," he said. "Have you been sick?"

She was trying to grope her way out of her fog, trying to grasp some reality in this insane situation. "Please tell me why you are here," she whispered.

"I told you. Yesterday after I finished some business that had me tied up all morning, I went over to your hotel. You had checked out. Left no word, no message for me. Just went."

He released her and began to move around the room in restless, angry strides. "The way it looked, you got the contracts, the thing you've been after, and hightailed it for home." He swung around, impaling her with his blazing eyes. "No matter how I try to figure it, I keep coming up with that same answer. You played up to me, put on a great, sexy act with me, gave me the big eye and the sweet talk and then when you got what you came after, you beat it out of Nashville without so much as a 'So long, Jess, you sucker! Nice knowing you.'"

She gasped and took a step backward as if he'd slapped her. "How dare you make such an accusation!"

He ran his fingers through his hair. His voice lost the

cutting edge. "Well, dammit, I don't want to think those things, Andrea. But what else was I to believe?"

"You might believe the truth!" she cried, suddenly feeling the release of pent-up fury exploding within her. "That is, if you know the truth when you see it. Maybe you're one of those pathological liars who lie so easily they forget what the truth is."

He stared at her with a black frown. "Would you care to explain that statement?"

"Certainly. I told you on the bus coming back from Knoxville that I'd learned the truth about you and Nori. But did you admit it like a man? Oh, no! You went into your lying routine, giving me that fairy story about letting Nori live at Skyland because you were being so magnanimous, such a big, helping friend. You lied so convincingly that you had me believing it! How smug you must have felt. How you must have been laughing at me!"

He shook his head, his expression growing darker. "But that's the truth."

"Oh? And what is that big, flashy rock on Nori's finger? A figment of my imagination?"

"I don't know what you're talking about!"

"Don't start that with me again, Jess Clark!" she said furiously. "I know Nori came from your hometown. I know she's been your woman for a long time. I know you've finally decided to do the decent thing about the poor child. I know yesterday morning you gave Nori the engagement ring and proposed and I know you are going to marry her right after the entertainer of the year award ceremony."

He was looking at her, his expression strange. "Nori told you that?"

"Yes."

"When?"

"When she brought me the signed contracts yesterday morning."

"Nori brought you the contracts?"

"Well, of course. You had her deliver them, didn't you?"

He shook his head slowly. "I gave them to my business manager's secretary and asked her to have them delivered along with the message that I'd see you after lunch. Nori must have happened to stop by the office and talked with the secretary and offered to take them to you herself. Andrea, there's not one word of truth in what Nori told you except for the part about coming from my hometown. Yes, that much is true. I knew her folks well. In fact, her dad worked in the mines with me. I was a green kid, scared and dumb. He taught me how to survive down there. Nori was a little kid in rompers then. When she grew up and came to Nashville, I naturally felt obligated to help her in every way I could. She does have a lot of talent, if she'd ever get her head on straight. You talk about pathological liars! That description sure fits Nori!"

Andrea strained to breathe. Her head felt like a balloon that was going to burst any minute. She put her hands over her ears. "Stop it! I don't believe one word of what you're saying. It's just like on the bus. You're trying to get me confused."

"But it's the truth."

"Then explain Nori's engagement ring!"

"I can't explain it. I don't know where she got it. Maybe it's one of those imitation diamonds she picked up somewhere. They can look pretty convincing. Nori can be a conniving little female. I know she's got her cap set for me. I've tried to make her understand I don't feel that way about her. I just wanted to help her. I guess she got real jealous over the attention I was paying you and embroidered up that little story hoping you'd believe it, grab the contract and head for the nearest plane home—which you did!''

Tears began trickling down Andrea's cheeks. "Jess, don't do this to me, please. Who am I to believe? Nori or you? I know you've wanted me since the moment we met. You've made that clear from the beginning. Nori said that I was a different kind of challenge from the kind of women you've been consorting with. You have a giant ego, Jess Clark. My running away from Nashville, turning you down cold, might have made the challenge even greater, might have inflamed your ego so you became more determined than ever to have me and so followed me down here. That's the real truth, isn't it?''

She felt she was teetering on the ragged edge of hysteria.

Jess crossed the room in two strides, towering over her again, his dark-eyed gaze enveloping her like a hot blanket. "Yes, I want you, Andrea," he said huskily. "And you want me. Even now when you're so angry, I know you want me. That's the truth, too, isn't it?''

He touched her arms and as if in reply to his relentless question, a tremor went through her body. Her knees weakened. She swayed toward him. She shook her head, swallowing painfully. "Leave me alone, Jess. Go back to Nori.''

"There's nothing to go back to. What do I have to do to

convince you? How does this sound? Marry me, Andrea.''

The blood drained from her cheeks. ''What?''

''Yes, I mean it. We can catch a flight to Las Vegas
today. By tonight you can be Mrs. Jess Clark. Now does
that sound like I've been lying? I couldn't very well marry
Nori if I'm married to you, now, could I?''

Andrea felt as if her knees would buckle. His closeness
was driving her out of her mind. She moved away from
him, trying to marshal her ragged thoughts. Jess had
proposed? Was she dreaming?

He moved closer again, catching her arms.

''Don't . . . please. . . .'' she whimpered.

But he refused to let her go. He drew her closer. His
body burned through the clothing against hers. She felt the
desire coming up in hot, pounding waves. Dimly she
heard herself whispering, ''No . . . no . . . no. . . .''
But it was to herself, not to Jess. To him, her body had its
own message: ''Yes . . . yes . . . yes!'' Where he
touched her were trails of fire. He put his finger under her
chin, raising her face to his. The power of his dark eyes
surged into the innermost depths of her being and held her
transfixed. His lips were on hers in a seeking, caressing
kiss that brought a quivering response.

Her cheeks were wet. Something Nori said echoed in
her ears. *Jess Clark would do anything, say anything, tell
any kind of lie to get something once he's made up his
mind he wants it.*

Would that include going so far as a hasty Las Vegas
wedding? Why not—if he saw there was no other way he
was going to get her! A marriage could be a temporary

thing, a means to an end, a way to satisfy his burning ego, and once satisfied, he had a team of lawyers to untie the knot.

She had no way of knowing the truth about Jess Clark, because she did not know what really went on in his heart. He was not a man who could open up about his deeper feelings. That inner core of Jess Clark was still a total stranger to her. Could she take this kind of a chance with a stranger?

He was kissing her again, his hands roaming over her in growing intimacy. Her thoughts became chaotic. How could she think when he was arousing such primitive passions, when her whole body was a throbbing vortex, when desire boiled in her like the molten lava of an aroused volcano?

He slipped open the buttons of her blouse, his fingers searching for the hidden secrets of twin delicate mounds. She gasped for breath, her body straining against his. Blood surged through her veins in pounding currents. She longed for him, yearned to surrender to him, hungered for completion with him.

She knew that with Jess Clark she would become more of a woman than she had ever dreamed possible. He had awakened hungers in her that she never dreamed had existed. He could unleash forces in her that would drive her to unbearable heights of ecstasy.

Against that, how could reason prevail?

"We're going to Las Vegas, right?" he whispered in her hair.

Andrea nodded.

Chapter Fifteen

Andrea sighed and stirred, looking around as she slowly awoke. The sight that met her eyes was a setting of luxurious comfort. Everything about the room reflected costly elegance—the plush furniture, the thick pile carpeting, the heavy drapes that hid them from the desert sun. It was the kind of costly Las Vegas hotel that millionaire corporate executives and big-name show people like Jess Clark could afford.

She propped herself up on an elbow and gazed at the man sleeping beside her. In the subdued light of the curtained room, Jess's suntanned features appeared almost swarthy. Her skin was milk white by comparison.

She trailed a finger over his forehead, playing with that rebellious lock of hair that never wanted to stay in place. Her finger traced a pattern down to the corner of his lips and a delicious little shiver ran through her. Jess stirred, murmured something unintelligible and went on sleeping.

The expression in her eyes as she gazed at the man she had married reflected the troubled uncertainty that clouded her mind. She wondered if she had dreamed the past twenty-four hours.

She lay back and held up her left hand. The wedding band on her ring finger was real enough.

Snatches of memory played across the screen in her mind: the hasty packing; the stop at the hospital to break the news to her grandfather; the flight across desert plains and the Continental Divide; the glitter and tinsel of the Las Vegas strip; the enormous signs flashing names of glamour stars against the desert night; the brief, contrived ceremony in the Hearts and Flowers Chapel. She remembered trying to suppress a giggle at the plastic, assembly-line artificiality. The only real thing about it was the fact that her left shoe pinched.

There had been a sumptuous dinner in one of the glamour palaces on the strip where only a few months ago Jess's name had blazed from the two-story sign outside.

Then he had carried her across the threshold of this room. She'd had the impression of entering a rose garden. Jess had made a quick call to a florist. Red roses were everywhere, dozens and dozens, even scattered across the giant king-size bed with its golden satin sheets.

Now she slid her bare legs from under the sheets. Quietly she slipped out of bed and padded into the bathroom, which was larger than most motel rooms. She was surrounded by gleaming tile, golden faucets, wall-length mirrors, satin-covered vanity seats. The whirlpool sunken bath on a raised tile dais was in the shape of a heart and was flanked by mirrors, creating a repeating reflection on both sides that seemed to extend into infinity. When she stepped into the warm, swirling water, she saw dozens of gradually diminishing reflections of herself on both sides.

She relaxed as the invisible fingers of water massaged her body. Closing her eyes, she surrendered to the sensation.

Her thoughts strayed back to her grandfather, the expression on his face yesterday when they'd stopped in at the hospital.

Nervous and embarrassed, she had introduced them. Jess had surprised Andrea by exhibiting a bit of formal, old-fashioned protocol. He had said, "Sir, I want to ask your permission to marry your granddaughter."

She had given Jess a grateful look, thanking him for understanding the old-world formality that was important to her grandfather.

"Married?" the old man had said with a look of bewilderment.

"Abuelo, I know this is a surprise and it's sudden. But I was with Jess a great deal while in Nashville. I—I do want to marry him. I know you want me to be happy."

"Yes, of course I do. But you didn't say a word about this to me. . . ."

The hurt expression on his face stabbed her. "Please forgive me, Abuelo. It—it has all happened so fast. I . . . I just wasn't able to talk about it. . . ."

The old man sighed and shook his head. "The young people these days. In my time it was different. Long courtships. The families had to know each other." He gave Jess a searching look. Then he said, "Andrea is like my own daughter. When her parents died, she came to live with me. I raised her. But she is a grown woman now. She has lived her own life for a number of years. If she were still under my roof, I might put my foot down. Under the circumstances, I can only wish the best and pray that God will go with you.''

Gravely he shook Jess's hand. ''I have been told that you are a good man, that you give many performances for charity and that you have religious convictions. Maybe it will be all right.''

Andrea hugged her grandfather tearfully.

The old man gave her a meaningful look. ''Have you told Raymond?''

She was sure he had guessed how deep Raymond's feelings for her went. ''I'll write Raymond a long letter from Las Vegas, explaining everything,'' she said. The last thing she wanted to do was hurt Raymond. But she would have hurt him even more if she'd held out any hope for him when she felt as she did about Jess Clark.

Before they left, Manola Castille thanked Jess for his agreement to participate in the promotion of Castille guitars. Jess assured him he would help all he could to keep the proud name of Castille alive. ''And thank you, sir, for the gift of the beautiful instrument. I'll treasure it.''

They parted in a spirit of goodwill. Andrea took with her the reassurance that her grandfather looked well on the road to recovery. The doctor had told him he would soon be released from the hospital and could resume normal activities.

Suddenly a noise brought her back to the present. Her

eyes flew open wide. Jess had come into the bathroom. He sat on the edge of the tub, dangling his legs in the water, gazing at her with a smile.

"Jess, quit looking at me that way," she said, self-consciously drawing up her knees and covering herself with her arms.

"What way?"

"You know."

"What's wrong with me looking at you?"

"You're embarrassing me!"

"But you're my wife now."

"I know. Give me time to get used to the idea. It's the first time I've had a man come into my bathroom when I was in the tub, naked."

"How about if I join you?"

"Jess!"

Despite her protests, he slid into the water. She felt the electrifying contact of his bare skin against hers."

"Jess . . ." Her voice grew thicker.

"Last night was great," he murmured in her ear, his breath stirring her hair. "Wasn't it?"

"Yes," she whispered, her voice trembling.

"I knew it would be. You were great."

"Jess—"

There were moments of silence with just the sound of the water bubbling softly around them.

"Jess . . ." Her breathing became heavy.

"Do you like that?"

"Ummm."

"And that?"

"Ummmmmmm. . . ."

More moments of silence. Through a kind of haze, she saw their reflections repeated over and over in the mirrors, her pale, soft white arms encircling his tanned neck.

Later, he carried her, still damp, into the bed with the golden satin sheets and they slept again for a while, arms around each other.

The days and nights melted together. They made love, they went to the casinos and the stage shows. They had champagne and lobster and thick steaks and crisp salads. Jess bought her a thousand dollars' worth of chips, which she lost at a roulette wheel, and she cried while he laughed. He rented a convertible and they rode out into the desert one night and, bathed in silver moonlight with mountains on the horizon and the perfume of desert plants in the air, they made love in the backseat like teenagers.

As Jess Clark's wife, she should have been the happiest woman in the world. But there was a growing sadness and emptiness within her.

Each hour she spent with Jess reinforced her love for him. But she was painfully aware that it was a love that was not returned. Jess talked about many things, about how satisfying the passion they shared was, what a great body she had, how much fun they had together. But the thing she longed to hear the most he never uttered. Not once, since the day he met her, had he used the word *love*. Never did he open up to her about his true feelings. Everything was surface. The real, inner Jess Clark was as much a stranger to her as he had been before she ever went to Nashville.

She felt alone and shut out.

She had a growing conviction that her suspicion had been right. As far as Jess was concerned she was no more than another conquest. He'd had to go to unusual and elaborate lengths to get what he wanted. But in the end he had triumphed.

The thrill of a fresh exploit would last for a while. A new bed partner, an unexplored passion, would keep him intrigued. Then the newness would wear off. Passion without love had a built-in time limit. Eventually he would tire of her and there would come the inevitable end.

At the end of the week they flew to Washington, D.C., for the award ceremony. Jess's eyes were bright with excitement. He talked about the rest of his group. "By now the bus will be on the road from Nashville. We'll get there a day early for rehearsal. . . ."

Andrea was thrilled for him and proud, but it was tempered with the lonely feeling of being an outsider.

On the night of the awards ceremony, Andrea was in the audience surrounded by VIPs from the world of show business and public life. It was a gala event. There was a stir of excitement and applause as the president of the United States and the first lady joined the audience with a contingent of Secret Service men and took their seats in a special box.

Andrea shook her head in amazement and wonder. Only in America could the son of a nameless coal miner be born in a mountain shack, quit school in the third grade to go to work, educate himself and eventually make such a success of his life that the entire nation including its president paid him homage.

Then the stage lights glared. The television cameras were on. There was an opening number by a large stage band. Then Andrea heard the voice of the master of ceremonies, the famous host of a night talk show that she had seen for years. "Friends, we are gathered here this evening for several reasons. First, this event culminates a week of celebration of our culture, the American culture, a culture which has taken its parts from a hundred other ethnic origins and fused them and uplifted them to a level like none other on this planet.

"That would be more than enough reason for us to be here. There is another, equally important. We're here to enjoy some of the best cotton-picking down-home music there is!"

There was a burst of laughter and applause. When it subsided, he continued, "Perhaps the best reason of all is to say thanks to a certain man, to do him honor and to give him a special award as the top country-western entertainer of the year.

"Now, this good ol' guitar picker would modestly say I'm only trying to butter him up if I say that he creates a masterpiece every time he cuts a recording. But it's true. His life is spent in enriching the lives of others through pure entertainment. But his kind of entertainment is more than that. This man, while filling us with joy through his music, has rediscovered the songs of our pioneering forefathers. He has taken us to the roots of America. He has written songs that remind us of a spirit of hope whatever the hardship, whether it be in a covered wagon trying to beat the winter snowfall to a mountain pass or in the dreams of a boy in a ghetto where, as an American, he can dare to hope."

"And here he is! I give you Mr. Jess Clark!"

Andrea sat in a strangely warm and pleasant paralysis as she heard the rising thunder of a standing ovation while

Jess came into the spotlight carrying his Castille guitar and looking absolutely elegant in black formal attire.

The ovation died and a hush settled over the auditorium. Jess spoke quietly and humbly in his soft drawl. "Folks, I guess it's true that America is the place to have dreams and I'm proof on the hoof. One dream after another has come true for me, from buying my first piece of music with money I earned shoveling coal to the early jobs in honky-tonks, to my first record and now to this award.

"I hope you'll forgive a little personal reference, because I want to tell the whole world that this week another wonderful dream came true for me. I want you all to know that I got married this week. The lady I married is . . . well, that's what she is, a real lady from a fine, aristocratic family. How she ever said yes to a barroom guitar picker like me has to be the good Lord's miracle.

"Now I'm just a country boy who grew up in Appalachia, the son of a dirt-poor coal miner. The way I was raised, us kids were taught from early on to keep our feelings to ourselves. The kind of people I grew up with don't talk much about what they feel inside. I never learned to say what was in my heart, except in a song. Mel Tillis, you know, stutters when he talks but never when he sings. I guess Mel would understand better than anybody else what I mean when I say that I can't talk it; I have to sing it.

"I've tried my best to tell this lady of mine how much she means to me, how far above me I think she is, how much I care for her and adore her and worship her, but the words just wouldn't come. I decided the only way I'm

ever going to be able to do it is in a song. So I've written a
new song especially for Andrea, just to tell her all the
things I feel for her in my heart, and I'm going to sing it
now, tonight, for the first time."

Dimly, Andrea heard the applause, felt the stares of a
whole nation as a spotlight found her and television
cameras turned her way. Tears streamed down her cheeks.

On the stage, backed by Peewee and Skeeter and Hooter
and Marilee, Jess began singing softly, "Lovin' you is all
I have to give you . . ."

Andrea sobbed with joy. She whispered, "Oh, Jess,
honey, that's all you'll ever have to give me from now on,
as long as we both live!"

Genuine Silhouette sterling silver bookmark for only $15.95!

What a beautiful way to hold your place in your current romance! This genuine sterling silver bookmark, with the distinctive Silhouette symbol in elegant black, measures 1½" long and 1" wide. It makes a beautiful gift for yourself, and for every romantic you know! And, at only $15.95 each, including all postage and handling charges, you'll want to order several now, while supplies last.

Send your name and address with check or money order for $15.95 per bookmark ordered to

Simon & Schuster Enterprises
120 Brighton Rd., P.O. Box 5020
Clifton, N.J. 07012
Attn: Bookmark

Bookmarks can be ordered pre-paid only. No charges will be accepted. Please allow 4-6 weeks for delivery.

N.Y. State Residents
Please Add Sales Tax